自领英语 轻悦读系列

温暖你的心

Warm Your Heart

邢洪君 等　编

内 容 提 要

本书精选了58篇英汉对照的英文亲情美文，从多个视角让爱永驻我们心中，同时可以提高读者对英文的驾驭能力。

本书适用于希望提高英语水平的广大英语爱好者日常学习和休闲阅读。

图书在版编目（CIP）数据

温暖你的心／邢洪君等编．—北京：中国水利水电出版社，2008

（白领英语轻悦读系列）

ISBN 978-7-5084-5483-2

Ⅰ．温…　Ⅱ．邢…　Ⅲ．①英语－汉语－对照读物②散文－作品集－世界　Ⅳ．H319.4：I

中国版本图书馆CIP数据核字（2008）第047219号

书　　名	白领英语轻悦读系列 **温暖你的心**
作　　者	邢洪君 等 编
出版发行	中国水利水电出版社（北京市三里河路6号　100044） 网址：www. waterpub. com. cn E-mail：sales@waterpub. com. cn 电话：(010) 63202266（总机）、68367658（营销中心）
经　　售	北京科水图书销售中心（零售） 电话：(010) 88383994、63202643 全国各地新华书店和相关出版物销售网点
排　　版	贵艺图文设计中心
印　　刷	北京市地矿印刷厂
规　　格	170mm×230mm　16开本　13.75印张　259千字
版　　次	2008年5月第1版　2008年5月第1次印刷
印　　数	0001—5000册
定　　价	**29.80**元（含光盘）

白领英语轻悦读系列

温暖你的心

主　编：邢洪君
编　委：邢洪君　段颖立　雷　涛　李云鹏
刘　恒　王　月　高　洁　韩伟民
毛　晗　赵国亚　郑崑琳　芦　涵
郭立萍　王福强　李宇环　艾　静
陈轶斐　郑　炎　郭　丹　郭宗炎
侯卫群

NTENTS

目　录

CONTENTS

NTENTS

CONTENTS

A Letter to the Son
写给儿子的信

Anonymous/佚名

Dear son…

孩子……

The day that you see me old and I am already not, have patience and try to understand me…

哪天你看到我日渐老去，身体也渐渐不行，请耐着性子试着了解我……

If I get dirty when eating… if I can not dress… have patience.

如果我吃得脏兮兮，如果我不会穿衣服……有耐心一点……

Remember the hours I spent teaching it to you.

你记得我曾花了多长时间教你这些事吗？

If, when I speak to you, I repeat the same things thousand and one times… do not interrupt me… listen to me.

如果，当我一再重复述说同样的事情……不要打断我，听我说……

When you were small, I had to read to you thousand and one times the same story until you get to sleep…

你小时候，我必须一遍又一遍地读着同样的故事，直到你静静地睡着……

When I do not want to have a shower, neither shame me nor scold me…

当我不想洗澡时，请不要羞辱我也不要责骂我……

Remember when I had to chase you with thousand excuses I invented, in order that you wanted to bath…

你记得小时候我曾用多少理由追促你，只为了哄你洗澡……

When you see my ignorance on new technologies… give me the necessary time and not look at me with your mocking smile…

当你看到我对新科技的无知，给我一点时间，不要挂着嘲弄的微笑看着我……

I taught you how to do so many things… to eat good, to dress well… to confront life…

我曾教了你多少事情啊……如何好好地吃，好好地穿…如何面对你的生命……

When at some moment I lose the memory or the thread of our conversation… let me have the necessary time to remember… and if I cannot do it, do not become nervous… as the most important thing is not my conversation but surely to be with you and to have you listening to me…

如果交谈中我忽然失忆不知所云，给我一点时间回想……

如果我还是无能为力，请不要紧张……

对我而言重要的不是对话，而是能跟你在一起，倾听我的诉说……

If ever I do not want to eat, do not force me. I know well when I need to and when not.

当我不想吃东西时，不要勉强我。我清楚地知道该什么时候进食。

When my tired legs do not allow me walk…

… give me your hand… the same way I did when you gave your first steps.

当我的腿不听使唤……扶我一把……

如同我曾扶着你踏出你人生的第一步……

And when someday I say to you that I do not want to live any more… that I want to die… do not get angry… some day you will understand…

Try to understand that my age is not lived but survived.

当哪天我告诉你我不想再活下去了……请不要生气……

总有一天你会了解……

试着了解我已是风烛残年。

Some day you will discover that, despite my mistakes, I always wanted the best thing for you.

有一天你会发现，即使我有许多过错，我总是尽我所能要给你最好的……

You must not feel sad, angry or impotent for seeing me near you. You must be next to me, try to understand me and to help me as I did it when you started living.

当我靠近你时不要觉得感伤，生气或无奈。

你要紧挨着我，如同我当初帮着你展开人生一样地了解我，帮我……

Help me to walk… help me to end my way with love and patience. I will pay you by a smile and by the immense love I have had always for you.

扶我一把，用爱跟耐心帮我走完人生……

我将用微笑和我始终不变的无边无际的爱来回报你。

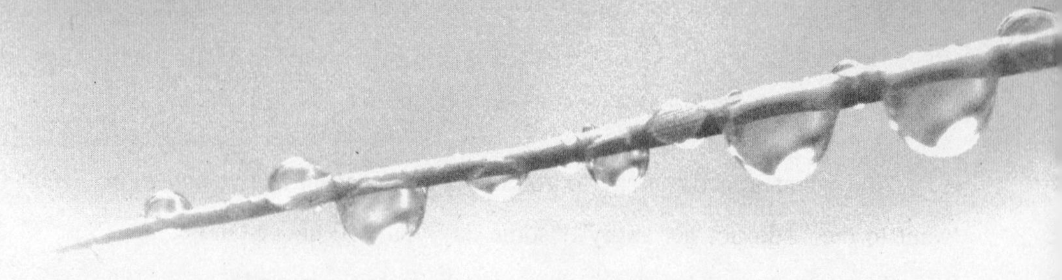

Women's Tears

女人的眼泪

Anonymous/佚名

A little boy asked his mother "why are you crying?"

一个男孩问他的妈妈："你为什么要哭呢?"

"Because I'm a woman," she told him.

妈妈说："因为我是女人啊。"

"I don't understand," he said.

男孩说："我不懂。"

His mum just hugged him and said, "and you never will."

他妈妈抱起他说："你永远不会懂得。"

Later the little boy asked his father, "Why does mother seem to cry for no reason?"

后来小男孩就问他爸爸："妈妈为什么毫无理由地哭呢?"

"All women cry for no reason," was all his dad could say.

"所有女人都这样。"他爸爸回答。

The little boy grew up and became a man, still wondering why women cry.

小男孩长成了一个男人，但仍旧不懂女人为什么哭泣。

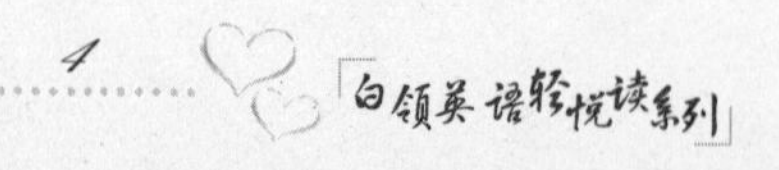

Finally he put in a call to god; and when god got on the phone, he asked, "God, why do women cry so easily?"

最后，他打电话给上帝；当上帝拿起电话时，他问道："上帝，女人为什么那么容易哭泣呢?"

God said: "when I made the woman she had to be special. I made her shoulders strong enough to carry the weight of the world; yet, gentle enough to give comfort."

上帝回答说："当我创造女人时，让她很特别。我使她的肩膀能挑起整个世界的重担，并且又足够温柔地给人慰藉。"

"I gave her an inner strength to endure childbirth and the rejection that many times comes from her children."

"我让她的内心很坚强，能够承受分娩的痛苦和忍受自己孩子多次的拒绝。"

"I gave her a hardness that allows her to keep going when everyone else gives up, and take care of her family through sickness and fatigue without complaining."

"我赋予她坚韧使她在别人放弃的时候继续坚持，并且无怨无悔地照顾自己的家人度过疾病和疲劳。"

"I gave her the sensitivity to love her children under any and all circumstances, even when her child has hurt her very badly."

"我赋予她感情使她……在任何情况下都会爱孩子，即使她的孩子伤害了她。"

"I gave her strength to carry her husband through his faults and fashioned her from his rib to protect his heart."

"我赋予她力量使她……包容她丈夫过错的坚强和用他的肋骨塑成她来保护他的心。"

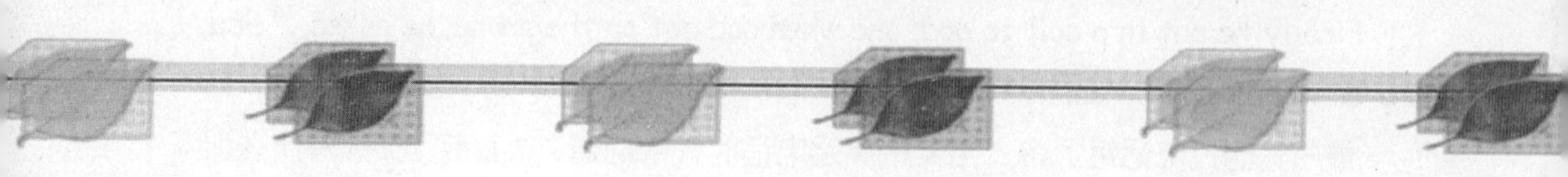

“I gave her wisdom to know that a good husband never hurts his wife, but sometimes tests her strengths and her resolve to stand beside him unfalteringly.”

“我赋予她智慧让她知道一个好丈夫是绝不会伤害他的妻子的，但有时会考验她支持自己丈夫的决心和坚强。”

“And finally, I gave her a tear to shed. This is hers exclusively to use whenever it is needed.”

“最后，我让她可以流泪。只要她愿意。这是她所独有的。”

“You see: the beauty of a woman is not in the clothes she wears, the figure that she carries, or the way she combs her hair.”

“你看，女人的漂亮不是因为她穿的衣服，她保持的体型或者她梳头的方式。”

“The beauty of a woman must be seen in her eyes, because that is the doorway to her heart the place where love resides.”

“女人的漂亮必须从她的眼睛中去看，因为那是她心灵的窗户和爱居住的地方。”

Home

家

Anonymous/佚名

What makes a home? Love and sympathy and confidence. It is a place where kindly affections exist among all the members of the family. The parents take good care of their children, and the children are interested in the activities of their parents. Thus all of them are bound together by affection, and they find their home to be the cheeriest place in the world.

A home without love is no more a home than a body without a soul is a man. Every civilized person is a social being. No one should live alone. A man may lead a successful and prosperous life, but prosperity alone can by no means insure happiness. Many great personages in the world history had deep affections for their homes.

Your home may be poor and humble, but duty lies there. You should try to make it cheerful and comfortable. The greater the difficulties, the richer will be your reward.

A home is more than a family dwelling. It is a school in which people are trained for citizenship. A man will not render good services to his country if he can do nothing good for his home; for in proportion as he loves his home, will he love his country. The home is the birthplace of true patriotism. It is the secret of social welfare and national greatness. It is the basis and origin of civilization.

组成家庭的因素是什么？答案即爱、同情和信赖。家是一个所有家庭成员凝结情感的地方。父母亲悉心照料孩子，而孩子们也对他们双亲的活动感兴趣。他们为爱所联结，因而发现家是世界上最令人感到欢乐的地方。

一个没有爱的家便不再称其为家，如同没有灵魂的躯体不再是人一样。每一个有修养的人都是社会性的人。没有人能够脱离社会独自生存。一个人也许过着成功而宽裕的生活，但是荣华富贵决不能保证幸福快乐。在世界历史上，许多名人都对其家庭怀有深情厚意。

你的家也许贫穷而简陋，但那正是你的职责所在。你应该努力使其愉快和舒适。你遭遇的困难越大，所得到的报偿也就越多。

家不仅仅是一个供家人居住的地方。它还是一个培养人们成为公民的场所。一个人假如无法对家庭做出有意义的事情，也就无法为国家提供优良的服务，因为爱家和爱国是成正比的。家庭是爱国主义精神的真正发源地，是社会福利和国家昌盛的秘诀，是文明的基础和起源。

A Father's Love

父亲的爱

Anonymous/佚名

Fathers seldom say "I love you"
父亲们很少说"我爱你"

Though the feeling's always there,
虽然那份感觉一直都在那儿,

But somehow those three little words
但不知道为什么这小小的三个字

Are the hardest ones to share.
却最难与人分享。

And fathers say "I love you"
而父亲说"我爱你"

In ways that words can't match —
用言语没法比拟的方式——

With tender bed time stories
或是温和地在床头讲故事

Or a friendly game of catch!
或是一场友好的捉迷藏游戏！

You can see the words "I love you"
你可以看到"我爱你"这些字

In a father's boyish eyes
从父亲孩子气的眼神里

When he runs home, all excited,
当他兴奋地跑回家，

With a poorly wrapped surprise.
脸上带着难以掩饰的惊喜。

A father says "I love you"
父亲说"我爱你"

With his strong helping hands
用他强有力的援助之手

With a smile when you're in trouble
用他的微笑帮你渡过难关

With the way he understands.
用他所理解的方式。

He says "I love you" haltingly
他踌躇地说"我爱你"

With awkward tenderness —
带着笨拙的温柔——

It's hard to help a four-year-old into a party dress!
帮一个四岁小孩穿上派对礼服实在是不容易！

He speaks his love unselfishly
他无私地表达他的爱

By giving all he can
付出他的全部

To make some secret dream come true.
让心底的梦想成真。

Or follow through a plan.
或追求一个计划。

A father's seldom-spoken love
父亲很少说出口的爱

Sounds clearly through the years —
随着光阴流逝变得清晰——

Sometimes in peals of laughter,
有时在响亮的笑声中，

Sometimes through happy tears.
有时在欢乐的泪水中。

Perhaps they have to speak their love
可能他们表达他们的爱

In a fashion all their own.
只能用自己的方式。

Because the love that fathers feel
因为父亲的爱

Is too big for words alone!
绝非言语所能诠释！

Your Angle

你的天使

Anonymous/佚名

Once upon a time there was a child ready to be born.

One day the child asked God, "They tell me you are going to send me to earth tomorrow but how am I going to live there being so small and helpless?"

God replied, "Among the many angels, I have chosen one for you. She will be waiting for you and will take care of you."

"But," said the child, "tell me here in Heaven I don't do anything else but sing and smile. That's what I need to be happy!"

God said, "Your angel will sing for you and will also smile for you every day. And you will feel your angel's love and be happy."

"And," said the child, how am I going to be able to understand when people talk to me, if I don't know the language that men talk?"

"That's easy", said God, "Your angel will tell you the most beautiful and sweet words you will ever hear, and with much patience and care, your angel will teach you how to speak."

The child looked up at God saying, "And what am I going to do when I want to talk to you?"

God smiled at the child saying, "Your angel will place your hands together and will teach you how to pray."

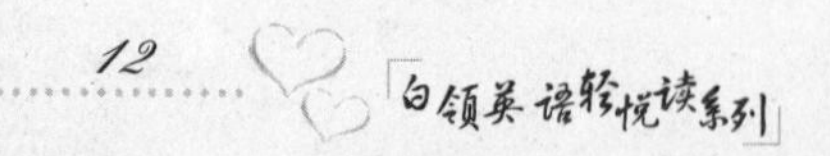

The child said, "I've heard on earth there are bad men. Who will protect me?"

God put his arm around the child, saying, "Your angel will defend you — even if it means risking life!"

The child looked sad saying, "But I will always be sad because I will not see you anymore."

God hugged the child, "Your angel will always talk to you about me and will teach you the way to come back to me, even though I will always be next to you."

At that moment there was much peace in heaven, but voices from earth could already be heard.

The child, in a hurry, asked softly, "Oh God, if I am about to leave now please tell me my angel's name!"

God replied, "Your angle's name is of no importance… you will simply call her MOMMY!"

有一个婴儿即将出生。

一天，这个小孩问上帝，“他们告诉我明天你将要把我送到地球，不过为什么我在那儿会那么小和无助呢？”

上帝说，“在所有的天使之中，我已经选中了一个给你。她将会等待你和照顾你。”

“不过，”小孩问了，“请告诉我——在天堂我除了歌唱和微笑之外什么都不做。这些是我快乐所需要的！”

上帝说，“你的天使每天将会为你歌唱和微笑。你将会感受到你的天使的爱，你会感到快乐。”

“还有，”小孩又问了，“如果我不懂他们说的语言，当人们对我说话的时候我怎样才会理解呢？”

“这很简单，”上帝说，“你的天使将教会你语言中最美丽和最甜蜜的词语，带着最大的耐心和关怀，你的天使将教会你怎样说话。”

小孩抬头看着上帝说，“我想和你说话的时候我该怎么做呢？”

上帝微笑着对小孩说，“你的天使会把你的双手放在一起然后教会你怎样祈祷。”

小孩说，“我听说地球上有坏人，谁将会保护我呢？”

上帝把手放在小孩身上，说，“你的天使将会保护你，甚至会冒生命的危险！”

小孩看起来有些悲伤，他说，“我将会一直感到悲伤因为我再也看不到你了。”上帝拥抱着小孩。“你的天使以后会一直跟你说有关我的事情，还会教你回到我身边的方法，虽说我一直与你同在。”

在这一刻小孩在天堂感到了无比的安详，不过已经可以听到从地球传来的声音。小孩有点焦急，温柔地问，“上帝啊，如果我现在将要离开，请告诉我我的天使的名字！”

上帝回答说，“你的天使的名字并不那么重要，你可以简单地叫她‘妈妈’！”

Mother
母亲的含义

Anonymous/佚名

"M" is for the million things she gave me,
"O" means only that she's growing old,
"T" is for the tears she shed to save me,
"H" is for her heart of purest gold,
"E" is for her eyes, with the love-light shining,
"R" means right, and right she'll always be.
Put them all together, they spell "MOTHER",
A word that means the world to me.

"M"代表她所给予我的无数，
"O"的意思是她在日渐老去，
"T"是她为抚育我洒下的泪，
"H"指她有像金子一般的心灵，
"E"是她的眼睛，洋溢着爱的光芒，
"R"的意思是正确，因为她永远都是对的。
将以上的字母串在一起就是"母亲"，
这个是我整个的世界。

A mother's love is like a circle, it has no beginning and ending. It keeps going around and around ever expanding, touching everyone who comes in touch with it. Engulfing them like the morning's mist, warming them like the noontime sun, and covering them like a blanket of evening stars. A mother's love is like a circle, it has no beginning and ending.

母爱就像一个圆环，没有起点也没有终点。它源源不绝，广阔无边，感染着每个接触到它的人。它如晨雾的笼罩，如正午太阳般温暖，又如夜星，照耀着人们。母爱就像一个圆环，没有起点也没有终点。

Circus
马戏表演前的一幕

Anonymous/佚名

Once, when I was a teenager, my father and I were standing in line to buy tickets for the circus. Finally, there was only one family between us and the ticket counter.

This family made a big impression on me. There were eight children, all probably under the age of 12. You could tell they didn't have a lot of money. Their clothes were not expensive, but they were clean. The children were well-behaved, all of them standing in line, two-by-two behind their parents, holding hands. They were excitedly jabbering about the clowns, elephants, and other acts they would see that night. One could sense they had never been to the circus before. It promised to be a highlight of their young lives. The father and mother were at the head of the pack, standing proud as could be.

The mother was holding her husband's hand, looking up at him as if to say, "You're my knight in shining armor." He was smiling and basking in pride, looking back at her as if to reply, "You got that right." The ticket lady asked the father how many tickets he wanted. He proudly responded, "Please let me buy eight children's tickets and two adult tickets so I can take my family to the circus." The ticket lady quoted the price. The man's wife let go of his hand, her head dropped, and his lip began to quiver. The father leaned a little closer and asked, "How much did you say?" The ticket lady again quoted the price. The man didn't have enough money. How was he supposed to turn and tell his eight kids that he didn't have enough money to take them to the circus?

Seeing what was going on, my dad put his hand in his pocket, pulled out a $20 bill and dropped it on the ground. (We were not wealthy in any sense of the word!) My father reached down, picked up the bill, tapped the man on the shoulder and said, "Excuse me, sir, this fell out of your pocket." The man knew what was going on. He wasn't begging for a handout but certainly appreciated the help in a desperate, heartbreaking, embarrassing situation. He looked straight into my dad's eyes, took my dad's hand in both of his, squeezed tightly onto the $20 bill, and with his lip quivering and a tear running down his cheek, he replied, "Thank you, thank you, sir. This really means a lot to me and my family."

My father and I went back to our car and drove home. We didn't go to the circus that night, but we didn't go without.

在我10多岁的时候，有一次父亲带我去看马戏团表演。当时排队买票的队伍很长。等了好长时间，终于我们前面只剩下一家人了。

这一家子给我的印象极深。他们有8个孩子，年龄估计都在12岁以下。显然这不会是一个富裕之家。他们衣着并不华贵，但也整洁体面。孩子们十分乖巧听话，两两一排，手牵手地排在双亲的身后。他们正兴高采烈、叽叽喳喳地讨论着马戏团里的小丑、大象等。凭感觉，这群孩子还从未看过马戏。所以，那可能是他们过得最精彩的一天。他们的父母亲排在最前面，昂首挺胸地站着。

那位母亲牵着丈夫的手，抬头看着他的脸，好像在说："你就是那穿着闪亮盔甲、保护我的骑士。"那位父亲微笑着，满脸自豪地看着妻子，像是在回答："你说对了。"售票小姐问他想买多少张票。他得意地回答说："请给我8张儿童票和两张成人票，我要带上全家去看马戏。"随后，售票小姐报了价钱。但那位母亲突然松开了握住丈夫的手，低下了头。而那位父亲的嘴唇开始颤抖起来，他往前靠了靠，问道："你刚才说多少钱？"售票小姐重复了一遍价格。他的钱不够。但是他要如何告诉那8个孩子说，他的钱不够让他们去看马戏呢？

这时，我父亲把手伸进了衣袋，掏出一张20美元，扔到了地上（我们绝不是什么有钱人！）。接着，爸爸弯下身又捡起了那张钞票，拍了拍前面那位父亲的肩膀，说："对不起，先生，这是从你口袋里掉出来的。"这位先生马上领会了其中的含义。他并不是在乞求施舍，但绝对会感激在这种绝望、伤心和尴尬的窘境向他伸出援手的人。他凝视着爸爸的眼睛，双手握着爸爸的手，攥紧了手里的那20美元。他的嘴唇又颤抖起来，一滴眼泪从脸颊滑落，他回答道，"谢谢，谢谢你，先生。您帮了我和我的全家一个大忙。"

最后，我和父亲开车折回了家。虽然那天晚上没有看成马戏，但是我们却没有白跑一趟。

If I Could Have Picked, I Would Have Picked You

如果能重新选择，我始终会选你

Anonymous/佚名

In the doorway of my home, I looked closely at the face of my 23-year-old son, Daniel, his backpack by his side. We were saying good-bye. In a few hours he would be flying to France. He would be staying there for at least a year to learn another language and experience life in a different country.

It was a transitional time in Daniel's life, a passage, a step from college into the adult world. I wanted to leave him some words that would have some meaning, some significance beyond the moment.

But nothing came from my lips. No sound broke the stillness of my beachside home. Outside, I could hear the shrill cries of sea gulls as they circled the ever changing surf on Long Island. Inside, I stood frozen and quiet, looking into the searching eyes of my son.

在家门口，我凝视着23岁的儿子丹尼尔的脸。他的背包就放在身旁。我们即将道别，几个小时之后，他就要飞往法国，在那里待上至少1年的时间。他要学习另一种语言，并在一个全新的国度体验新的生活。

这是丹尼尔生命中的一个过渡时期，也是他从象牙塔进入成人世界踏出的一步。我希望送给他几句话，几句能让他受用终身的话语。

但我竟一句话也说不出来。我们的房子坐落在海边，此刻屋里静寂无声。屋外，海鸥在波涛澎湃的长岛海域上空盘旋，我能听见它们发出的尖叫。我就这样站在屋里，默默地注视着儿子那双困惑的眼睛。

What does it matter in the course of a life-time if a father never tells a son what he really thinks of him? But as I stood before Daniel, I knew that it does matter. My father and I loved each other. Yet, I always regretted never hearing him put his feelings into words and never having the memory of that moment. Now, I could feel my palms sweat and my throat tighten. Why is it so hard to tell a son something from the heart? My mouth turned dry, and I knew I would be able to get out only a few words clearly.

"Daniel," I said, "if I could have picked, I would have picked you."

That's all I could say. I wasn't sure he understood what I meant. Then he came toward me and threw his arms around me. For a moment, the world and all its people vanished, and there was just Daniel and me in our home by the sea.

即使一位父亲一辈子都不曾亲口告诉儿子自己对他的看法，那又如何？然而，当我面对着丹尼尔，我意识到这非常重要。我爱我的父亲，他也爱我。但我从未听过他说心里话，更没有这些感人的回忆。为此，我总心怀遗憾。现在，我手心冒汗，喉咙打结。为什么对儿子说几句心里话如此困难？我的嘴唇变得干涩，我想我顶多能够清晰地吐出几个字而已。

"丹尼尔，"我终于迸出了一句，"如果上帝让我选择谁是我的儿子，我始终会选你。"

这是我唯一能想到的话了。我不能肯定他是否明白了我的意思。这时他走过来抱住了我。那一刻，世界消失了，只剩下我和丹尼尔站在海边的小屋里。

He was saying something, but my eyes misted over, and I couldn't understand what he was saying. All I was aware of was the stubble on his chin as his face pressed against mine. And then, the moment ended. I went to work, and Daniel left a few hours later with his girlfriend.

That was seven weeks ago, and I think about him when I walk along the beach on weekends. Thousands of miles away, somewhere out past the ocean waves breaking on the deserted shore, he might be scurrying across Boulevard Saint Germain, strolling through a musty hallway of the Louvre, bending an elbow in a Left Bank café.

What I had said to Daniel was clumsy and trite. It was nothing. And yet, it was everything.

丹尼尔也在说着什么，但泪水已经模糊了我的双眼，我一个字也没听进去。只是当他的脸向我贴过来时，我感觉到了他下巴的胡子茬。然后，一切恢复原样。我上班去了，丹尼尔几个小时后带着女友离开了。

7个星期过去了，周末在海边散步时我会想起丹尼尔。横跨拍打着荒芜海岸的茫茫大海，几千英里之外的某个地方，丹尼尔也许正飞奔着穿越圣热蒙大道，或者在罗浮宫散发着霉味的走廊上徘徊，又或者此时正托着下巴坐在左岸咖啡馆里憩息。

我对丹尼尔说的那些话既晦涩又老套，空洞无文。然而，它却道出了一切。

My Busy Day

我的繁忙日子

Anonymous/佚名

"Mommy, look!" cried my daughter, Darla, pointing to a chicken hawk soaring through the air.

"Uh huh," I murmured, driving, lost in thought about the tight schedule of my Day.

Disappointment filled her face. "What's the matter, Sweetheart?" I asked, entirely dense.

"Nothing," my seven-year-old said. The moment was gone. Near home, we slowed to search for the albino deer that comes out from behind the thick mass of trees in the early evening. She was nowhere to be seen.

"Tonight, she has too many things to do," I said.

Dinner, baths and phone calls filled the hours until bedtime.

"Come on, Darla, time for bed!" She raced past me up the stairs. Tired, I kissed her on the cheek, said prayers and tucked her in.

"妈妈，看!"我的女儿达拉喊到，小手指着翱翔在空中的小鹰。

当时我开着车，正想着我当天忙碌的日程安排，便随口“嗯“了一声。

女儿一脸的失望。“乖乖，怎么啦?”我问道，完全不知道发生了什么事。

“没什么，”我那7岁的女儿说道。那不愉快的一刻很快就过去了。快到家了，我放慢了车速，想找那头白化变种鹿。她通常在入夜时出现在那片茂密的树林里。但这次我们却找不到她的影踪。

“小鹿今晚太忙了，”我说。

晚餐，沐浴、电话占据了我睡觉前的所有时间。

“达拉，睡觉了!”她从我身旁跑过，我这时已觉得很疲惫，吻了吻她的脸，说了几句祷告的话后便把她推进房里去。

"Mom, I forgot to give you something!" she said. My patience was gone.

"Give it to me in the morning." I said, but she shook her head.

"You won't have time in the morning!" she retorted.

"I'll take time," I answered defensively. Sometimes no matter how hard I tried, time flowed through my fingers like sand in an hourglass, never enough. Not enough for her, for my husband, and definitely not enough for me.

She wasn't ready to give up yet. She wrinkled her freckled little nose in anger and swiped away her chestnut brown hair.

"No, you won't! It will be just like today when I told you to look at the hawk. You didn't even listen to what I said."

"妈，我忘了给你些东西!"她说。我当时已经没有耐性再听她说话了。

"明早再给我吧。"我说，但她却摇摇头。

"你明早没时间的!"她反驳道。

"我会抽时间的，"我辩解道。有时候，不管我怎么努力，时间还是像沙漏里的沙子一样从我的指间里流走，似乎永远不够用。我永远没有足够的时间花在女儿身上，丈夫身上，在自己身上更是如此。

她没打算放弃。她生气地皱了皱长着雀斑的小鼻子，拨弄了一下她那栗色的头发。

"不！你不会有时间的！就像今天我让你看看天上的小鹰的时候，你根本就没留意我在说什么。"

I was too weary to argue; she hit too close to the truth. "Good night!" I shut her door with a resounding thud.

Later though, her gray-blue gaze filled my vision as I thought about how little time we really had until she was grown and gone.

My husband asked, "Why so glum?" I told him.

"Maybe she's not asleep yet. Why don't you check?" he said with all the authority of a parent in the right. I followed his advice, wishing it was my own idea.

I cracked open her door, and the light from the window spilled over her sleeping form. In her hand I could see the remains of a crumpled paper. Slowly I opened her palm to see what the item of our disagreement had been.

Tears filled my eyes. She had torn into small pieces a big red heart with a poem she had written titled, "Why I Love My Mother!"

我太累了，不想跟她争论。她说得很对。“晚安!”我重重地关上了她的门。

夜深了，我眼前仍然浮现着女儿蓝灰色的眸子，我想到在女儿长大成人离开我们之前我们共处的时间已所剩无几。

“怎么这么惆怅呢?”我丈夫问。我跟他说了事情的来龙去脉。

“也许她还没睡着呢。为什么不去看看呢?”丈夫以一种完全家长式的语气说道。我接受了他的建议，想着这要是我自己的主意就好了。

我把门推开了一道小缝。透过窗户射进的光线刚好照在她身上。我看到她手上揣着张皱皱的纸。我慢慢地摊开她的手掌，想看看究竟是什么东西导致了我们母女的不和。

我的眼睛湿润了。她把一个大大的红心撕成了碎片，上面是她自己写的一首诗的诗名，“为什么我爱妈妈!”

I carefully removed the tattered pieces. Once the puzzle was put back into place, I read what she had written:

Why I Love My Mother

Although you're busy and you work so hard, you always take time to play I love you Mommy because I am the biggest part of your busy day!

The words were an arrow straight to the heart. At seven years old, she had the wisdom of Solomon.

Ten minutes later I carried a tray to her room, with two cups of hot chocolate with marshmallows and two peanut butter and jelly sandwiches. When I softly touched her smooth cheek, I could feel my heart burst with love.

Her thick dark lashes lay like fans against her lids as they fluttered, awakened from a dreamless sleep, and she looked at the tray.

"What is that for?" she asked, confused by this late-night intrusion.

"This is for you, because you are the most important part of my busy day!" She smiled and sleepily drank half her cup of chocolate. Then she drifted back to sleep, not really understanding how strongly I meant what I said.

我小心翼翼地拿走那些碎片，并重新拼凑起来。诗是这样写的：

为什么我爱妈妈

虽然你很忙，而且也做得很辛苦，但你总是抽时间陪我玩。我爱妈咪，因为我是你繁忙日子里最重要的部分！

女儿的话语像箭一样刺痛了我的心。7岁的她居然具备了所罗门的智慧。

10分钟后，我端着一个托盘走进她的房间，托盘上盛着两杯葵蜜饯热巧克力饮料，两片花生黄油和果冻三文治。轻抚着她的脸颊，我的心里盈满了爱意。

她眨着眼睛，乌黑浓密的睫毛像扇子一样在她睡意惺忪的脸颊上扇动，她看着我的托盘。

"这是给谁弄的？"她问道，对我这深夜的造访感到迷惑。

"是给你弄的，因为你是我繁忙日子里最重要的部分！"她笑了，睡意朦胧地喝了半杯巧克力饮料。然后便又躺下睡了，她并没听出我那句话里饱含的深情。

Mum's Letters

母亲的信

Anonymous/佚名

To this day I remember my mum's letters. It all started in December 1941. Every night she sat at the big table in the kitchen and wrote to my brother Johnny, who had been drafted that summer. We had not heard from him since the Japanese attacked Pearl Harbor.

I didn't understand why my mum kept writing Johnny when he never wrote back.

"Wait and see — we'll get a letter from him one day," she claimed. Mum said that there was a direct link from the brain to the written word that was just as strong as the light God has granted us. She trusted that this light would find Johnny.

I don't know if she said that to calm herself, dad or all of us down. But I do know that it helped us stick together, and one day a letter really did arrive. Johnny was alive on an island in the Pacific.

至今我依然记得母亲的信。事情要从1941年12月说起。母亲每晚都坐在厨房的大饭桌旁边，给我弟弟约翰写信。那年夏天约翰应征入伍。自从日本袭击珍珠港以后，他就一直杳无音信。

约翰从未回信，我不明白母亲为何还要坚持写下去。

可母亲还是坚持说："等着瞧吧，总有一天他会给我们回信的。"她深信思想和文字是直接相连，这种联系就像上帝赋予人类的光芒一样强大，而这道光芒终会照耀到约翰的身上。

虽然我不肯定她是否只是在安慰自己，或是父亲，或者是我们几个孩子，但我们一家人却因此更加亲密。而最终我们终于等到了约翰的回信，原来他驻扎在太平洋的一个岛屿上，安然无恙。

Whenever mum had finished a letter, she gave it to dad for him to post it. Then she put the water on to boil, and we sat down at the table and talked about the good old days when our Italian-American family had been a family of ten: mum, dad and eight children. Five boys and three girls. It is hard to understand that they had all moved away from home to work, enrolled in the army, or got married. All except me.

Around next spring mum had got two more sons to write to. Every evening she wrote three different letters which she gave to me and dad afterwards so we could add our greetings.

"All people in this world are here with one particular purpose," she said. "Apparently, mine is to write letters." She tried to explain why it absorbed her so.

每次母亲写完信，就会把信交给父亲去邮寄。然后她把水烧开，和我们围坐在桌旁，聊聊过去的好日子。从前我们这个意裔的美国家庭可是人丁兴旺：父母亲和我们8个兄弟姐妹——5男3女，济济一堂。现在他们都因工作、入伍或婚姻纷纷离开了家，只有我留下来，想想真觉匪夷所思。

第二年春天，母亲也要开始给另外两个儿子写信了。每天晚上，她先写好3封内容不同的信交给我和父亲，然后我们再加上自己的问候。

母亲试着解释她为何如此沉迷写信，"每个人来到这个世界都有一个目的。显然，我就是来写信的。"

"A letter unites people like nothing else. It can make them cry, it can make them laugh. There is no caress more lovely and warm than a love letter, because it makes the world seem very small, and both sender and receiver become like kings in their own kingdoms. My dear, a letter is life itself!"

Today all mum's letters are lost. But those who got them still talk about her and cherish the memory of her letters in their hearts.

"信无可替代地把人与人连在一起，让人笑，让人哭。一封充满爱的信比任何爱抚更令人觉得亲爱和温暖，因为它让世界变小，写信人和收信人都成为自己世界里的国王。亲爱的，信就是生命本身！"

今天，母亲所有的信已经遗失。但是那些收到信的人仍在谈论她，并把有关信的记忆珍藏在心。

Apple Tree

苹果树

A long time ago, there was a huge apple tree. A little boy loved to come and lay around it every day. He climbed to the tree top, ate the apples, took a nap under the shadow… He loved the tree and the tree loved to play with him.

很久很久以前，有一棵又高又大的苹果树。一位小男孩，天天到树下来，他爬上去摘苹果吃，在树荫下睡觉。他爱苹果树，苹果树也爱和他一起玩耍。

Time went by… the little boy had grown up and he no longer played around the tree every day. One day, the boy came back to the tree and he looked sad. "Come and play with me," the tree asked the boy. "I am no longer a kid, I don't play around trees anymore." The boy replied, "I want toys. I need money to buy them." "Sorry, but I don't have money… but you can pick all my apples and sell them. So, you will have money." The boy was so excited. He grabbed all the apples on the tree and left happily. The boy never came back after he picked the apples. The tree was sad.

后来，小男孩长大了，不再天天来玩耍。一天他又来到树下，很伤心的样子。苹果树要和他一起玩，男孩说："不行，我不小了，不能再和你玩，我要玩具，可是没钱买。"苹果树说："很遗憾，我也没钱，不过，把我所有的果子摘下来卖掉，你不就有钱了?"男孩十分激动，他摘下所有的苹果，高高兴兴地走了。然后，男孩好久都没有来。苹果树很伤心。

One day, the boy returned and the tree was so excited. "Come and play with me," the tree said. "I don't have time to play. I have to work for my family. We need a house for shelter. Can you help me?" "Sorry, but I don't have a house. But you can chop off my branches to build your house." So the boy cut all the branches off the tree and left happily. The tree was glad to see him happy but the boy never came back since then. The tree was again lonely and sad.

有一天，男孩终于来了，树兴奋地邀他一起玩。男孩说：“不行，我没有时间，我要替家里干活呢，我们需要一幢房子，你能帮忙吗?”“我没有房子，”苹果树说，“不过你可以把我的树枝统统砍下来，拿去搭房子。”于是男孩砍下所有的树枝，高高兴兴地运走去盖房子。看到男孩高兴树好快乐。从此，男孩 又不来了。树再次陷入孤单和悲伤之中。

One hot summer day, the boy returned and the tree was delighted. “Come and play with me!” the tree said. “I am sad and getting old. I want to go sailing to relax myself. Can you give me a boat?” “Use my trunk to build your boat. You can sail far away and be happy.” So the boy cut the tree trunk to make a boat. He went sailing and never showed up for a long time. The tree was happy, but it was not true.

一年夏天，男孩回来了，树太快乐了：“来呀！孩子，来和我玩呀。”男孩却说：“我心情不好，一天天老了，我要扬帆出海，轻松一下，你能给我一艘船吗?”苹果树说：“把我的树干砍去，拿去做船吧!”于是男孩砍下了她的树干，造了条船，然后驾船走了，很久都没有回来。树好快乐……但不是真的。

Finally, the boy returned after he left for so many years. “Sorry, my boy. But I don't have anything for you anymore. No more apples for you…” the tree said.

“I don't have teeth to bite.” the boy replied.

许多年过去，男孩终于回来，苹果树说：“对不起，孩子，我已经没有东西可以给你了，我的苹果没了。”

男孩说：“我的牙都掉了，吃不了苹果了。”

“No more trunk for you to climb on.”

“I am too old for that now.” the boy said.

“I really can't give you anything… the only thing left is my dying roots.” the tree said with tears.

苹果树又说：“我再没有树干，让你爬上来了。”

男孩说：“我太老了，爬不动了。”

“我再也没有什么给得出手了……，只剩下枯死下去的老根。”树流着泪说。

“I don't need much now, just a place to rest. I am tired after all these years.” The boy replied.

“Good! Old tree roots is the best place to lean on and rest. Come, Come sit down with me and rest.” The boy sat down and the tree was glad and smiled with tears...

男孩说：“这么多年过去了，现在我感到累了，什么也不想要，只要一个休息的地方。”

“好啊！老根是最适合坐下来休息的，来啊，坐下来和我一起休息吧。”男孩坐下来，苹果树高兴得流下了眼泪……

This is a story of everyone. The tree is our parent. When we were young, we loved to play with Mom and Dad... When we grown up, we left them, and only came to them when we need something or when we are in trouble. No matter what, parents will always be there and give everything they could to make you happy. You may think that the boy is cruel to the tree but that's how all of us are treating our parents.

这就是我们每个人的故事。这颗树就是我们的父母。小时候，我们喜欢和爸爸妈妈玩……长大后，我们就离开他们，只在需要什么东西或者遇到麻烦的时候，才回到他们身边。无论如何，父母永远都在那儿，倾其所有使你快乐。你可能认为这个男孩对树很残酷，但这就是我们每个人对待父母的方式。

Christmas Story
圣诞节的故事

Anonymous/佚名

One afternoon about a week before Christmas, my family of four piled into our minivan to run an errand, and this question came from a small voice in the back seat: "Dad," began my five-year-old son, Patrick, "how come I've never seen you cry?"

Just like that. No preamble. No warning. Surprised, I mumbled something about crying when he wasn't around, but I knew that Patrick had put his young finger on the largest obstacle to my own peace and contentment — the dragon-filled moat separating me from the fullest human expression of joy, sadness and anger. Simply put, I could not cry.

在圣诞节前一个星期的某个下午，我们一家四口人挤进自己家的小货车去送货，车后座忽然轻声地传来这样一个问题："爸爸，"我5岁的儿子——帕特里克开始问道："我怎么从来没见你哭过呢?"

就是这么唐突，没有前言，没有任何的预示。我感到很错愕，当他不在一旁时，我自言自语地琢磨着哭泣这一话题，但我知道帕特里克那小脑袋已经发现了我心灵深处的一道屏障，那道屏障使我无法获得内心的平静与满足，像一道难以逾越的壕沟，把我从充满人性感情的喜悦、悲哀和生气中隔离开来。直接一点说，我就是不能哭。

I am scarcely the only man for whom this is true. We men have been conditioned to believe that stoicism is the embodiment of strength. We have traveled through life with stiff upper lips, secretly dying within.

For most of my adult life I have battled depression. Doctors have said much of my problem is physiological, and they have treated it with medication. But I know that my illness is also attributable to years of swallowing rage, sadness, even joy.

Strange as it seems, in this world where macho is everything, drunkenness and depression are safer ways for men to deal with feelings than tears. I could only hope the same debilitating handicap would not be passed to the next generation.

So the following day when Patrick and I were in the van after playing at a park, I thanked him for his curiosity. Tears are a good thing, I told him, for boys and girls alike. Crying is God's way of healing people when they're sad. "I'm glad you can cry whenever you're sad," I said. "Sometimes daddies have a harder time showing how they feel. Someday I hope to do better."

其实这种情况并不是只发生在我身上。我们男人已经接受了这种信念，坚忍克己才是力量的体现。在人生道路上，我们总是抿着僵硬的上唇，丝毫不让自己有任何的感情外露，内心的情感不知不觉中已枯竭。

成年后的大部分日子我都在与消沉沮丧抗争。医生都说我的问题主要是生理上的，所以他们给我作药物治疗。但我知道，我的病根在于我多年来对愤怒、悲哀，甚至是欢乐等情感的压抑。

但这似乎也很奇怪，在雄性主宰一切的世界里，男人在处理感情困扰时，酗酒和消沉是比痛哭流涕更安全的方法。我只是希望这种耗损人精神体力的情感障碍不会传给下一代。

所以，第二天，我带帕特里克去公园玩，在驾车返家途中，我对他的好奇表示了谢意。我告诉他：无论对于男孩还是女孩，流眼泪都是件好事情。哭泣是当人们悲哀时，上帝拯救他们的方法。“我很高兴，在你觉得伤心的时候，你都能哭出来，”我说，“有时候做爸爸的比较难以表达他们的情感。我希望有一天我会做得更好。”

Patrick nodded. In truth, I held out little hope. But in the days before Christmas I prayed that somehow I could connect with the dusty core of my own emotions.

"I was wondering if Patrick would sing a verse of 'Away in a Manger' during the service on Christmas Eve," the church youth director asked in a message left on our answering machine.

My wife, Catherine, and I struggled to contain our excitement. Our son's first solo.

Catherine delicately broached the possibility, reminding Patrick how beautifully he sang, telling him how much fun it would be. Patrick himself seemed less convinced and frowned. "You know, mom," he said, "sometimes when I have to do something important, I get kind of scared."

帕特里克点点头。事实上，我对此不抱什么希望。但圣诞节前的那些日子里，我祈祷着无论如何也要揭开我那尘封的感情了。

"不知道帕特里克是否愿意在平安夜的礼拜仪式上唱《远处的马槽》这首圣诗呢，"教堂里主管年轻教徒的神甫在我们的电话留言里问道。

我的妻子凯瑟琳和我都拼命地抑制着内心的兴奋。这是我们的儿子第一次独唱。

凯瑟琳很巧妙地向帕特里克问及这件事的可能性。她提醒帕特里克，他的歌唱得有多动听，告诉他那是多么有趣的事。帕特里克似乎不大相信这些话，他皱着眉头。"你知道的，妈妈，"他说，"有时候，当我要做一件重要的事情时，我总觉得害怕。"

Grownups feel that way too, he was assured, but the decision was left to him. His deliberations took only a few minutes.

"Okay," Patrick said. "I'll do it."

From the time he was an infant, Patrick has enjoyed an unusual passion for music. By age four he could pound out several bars of Wagner's *Ride of the Valkyries* on the piano.

For the next week Patrick practiced his stanza several times with his mother. A rehearsal at the church went well. Still, I could only envision myself at age five, singing into a microphone before hundreds of people. When Christmas Eve arrived, my expectations were limited.

Catherine, our daughter Melanie and I sat with the congregation in darkness as a spotlight found my son, standing alone at the microphone. He was dressed in white, with a pair of angel wings.

Slowly, confidently, Patrick hit every note. As his voice washed over the people, he seemed a true angel, a true bestower of Christmas miracles.

我们告诉他大人也有这样的感觉，但最后还得由他自己决定。他只沉思了几分钟。

"好吧，"帕特里克说，"我去。"

打从襁褓开始，帕特里克就对音乐表现出不同寻常的热爱。他4岁时，就能在钢琴上敲出瓦格纳的《女武神》的几个小节了。

在接下来的那个星期，帕特里克和他的妈妈把那首圣诗练习了好几次。在教堂里举行的彩排非常成功。相比起来，在我5岁的时候只能想象自己在数百人面前对着麦克风歌唱。而当平安夜到来的时候，我的期望就会落空。

凯瑟琳、我们的女儿梅拉尼、我和其他的信众坐在黑暗当中，当一盏聚光灯掠过时，我找到了我儿子，他一个人站在麦克风前面，白衣飘飘，两侧插着天使的翅膀。

缓缓地、自信地，帕特里克唱准了每一个音符。他的声音陶醉了在座的每一个人，他就像是一个真正的天使，上帝赐予的一件奇迹般的圣诞礼物。

There was eternity in Patrick's voice that night, a beauty rich enough to penetrate any reserve. At the sound of my son, heavy tears welled at the corners of my eyes.

His song was soon over, and the congregation applauded. Catherine brushed away tears. Melanie sobbed next to me.

After the service, I moved to congratulate Patrick, but he had more urgent priorities. "Mom," he said as his costume was stripped away, "I have to go to the bathroom."

As Patrick disappeared, the pastor wished me a Merry Christmas, but emotion choked off my reply. Outside the sanctuary I received congratulations from fellow church members.

I found my son as he emerged from the bathroom. "Patrick, I need to talk to you about something," I said, smiling. I took him by the hand and led him into a room where we could be alone. I knelt to his height and admired his young face, the large blue eyes, the dusting of freckles on his nose and cheeks, the dimple on one side.

那晚，帕特里克的声音里似乎蕴含着永恒，他的声音圆润得足以穿透世间万物。聆听着儿子的歌声，大颗大颗的泪珠从我眼角涌了出来。

他的歌很快唱完了，大家都鼓起掌来。凯瑟琳擦拭着眼泪，梅拉尼在我身旁哽咽。

礼拜结束后，我去向帕特里克道贺，但他却急着做别的事情。"妈妈，"他一边脱衣服一边说，"我得先去洗手间。"

帕特里克走开后，牧师祝我圣诞快乐，但我激动得一句话也答不上来。在教堂外，我接受了信众们的祝贺。

我找到了我的儿子，当时他正从洗手间出来。"帕特里克，我要和你谈谈。"我微笑着说。我拉着他的手，带他到一个只有我们俩的房间。我蹲下来，和他一般高，欣赏着他那嫩嫩的脸蛋，蓝色的大眼睛，鼻子和两颊上有一层雀斑，一边面颊上还有一个小酒窝。

He looked at my moist eyes quizzically.

"Patrick, do you remember when you asked me why you had never seen me cry?"

He nodded.

"Well, I'm crying now."

"Why, Dad?"

"Your singing was so wonderful it made me cry."

Patrick smiled proudly and flew into my arms.

"Sometimes," my son said into my shoulder, "life is so beautiful you have to cry."

他不解地看着我湿润的双眼。

"帕特里克，你还记得你问过我为什么没有见过我哭吗?"

他点点头。

"嗯，我在哭呢。"

"为什么呢，爸爸?"

"因为你的歌唱得太好了。"

帕特里克自豪地笑着扑进我的怀抱。

"有时候，"我儿子伏在我肩膀上说，"生活会美得让你流泪。"

Our moment together was over too soon. Untold treasures awaited our five-year-old beneath the tree at home, but I wasn't ready for the traditional plunge into Christmas just yet. I handed Catherine the keys and set off for the mile-long hike home.

The night was cold and crisp. I crossed a park and admired the full moon hanging low over a neighborhood brightly lit in the colors of the season. As I turned toward home, I met a car moving slowly down the street, a family taking in the area's Christmas lights. Someone rolled down a window.

"Merry Christmas," a child's voice yelled out to me.

"Merry Christmas," I yelled back. And the tears began to flow all over again.

我们在一起的瞬间太短暂了。家中圣诞树下的那些神秘的礼物正等着我5岁的儿子，但我还没有为一贯以来都匆匆而来的圣诞节做好准备。我把车钥匙递给凯瑟琳，徒步走回1英里以外的家。

那晚的天气干燥寒冷。我穿过公园，在这多彩而快乐的时节，欣赏着挂在半空的满月照耀着万家灯火。当转身回家时，我看见一辆车在街上慢慢地行驶着，原来是一家人在欣赏区内的圣诞灯饰。有人拉下了窗户。

"圣诞快乐。"一个小孩对着我喊。

"圣诞快乐。"我回应道。眼泪又开始流出来了。

Revenge

报 复

Anonymous/佚名

My grandmother was an iron-willed woman, the feared matriarch of our New York family back in the 1950s.

When I was five years old, she invited some friends and relatives to her Bronx apartment for a party. Among the guests was a neighborhood big shot who was doing well in business. His wife was proud of their social status and let everyone at the party know it. They had a little girl about my age who was spoiled and very much used to getting her own way.

Grandmother spent a lot of time with the big shot and his family. She considered them the most important members of her social circle and worked hard at currying their favor.

20世纪50年代我们家住在纽约，当时祖母是一家之主，也是一个令人敬畏的强悍女人。

我5岁那年，她邀请了一些亲戚朋友到布朗克斯的公寓里聚会。在客人中有个做生意发了财的大款，他的妻子神气地向大家炫耀他们家的社会地位。他们有个娇气的小女儿，年纪跟我差不多，脾气很蛮横。

祖母殷勤地伺候着那个大款和他的家人，她把他们看作是她的社交圈里最重要的人物，因此她不遗余力地逢迎他们。

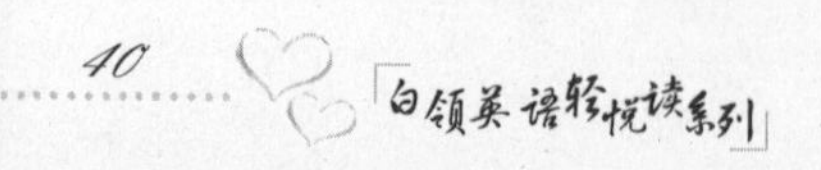

At one point during the party, I made my way to the bathroom and closed the door behind me. A minute or two later, the little girl opened the bathroom door and grandly walked in. I was still sitting down.

"Don't you know that little girls aren't supposed to come into the bathroom when a little boy is using it!?" I hollered.

The surprise of my being there, along with the indignation I had heaped upon her, stunned the little girl. Then she started to cry. She quickly closed the door, ran to the kitchen, and tearfully complained to her parents and my grandmother.

Most of the partygoers had overheard my loud remark and were greatly amused by it. But not Grandmother.

晚会进行中，我走进了洗手间并随手把门关上。大概一两分钟后，我当时还坐在马桶上，那个小女孩推开洗手间的门，大模大样地走了进来。

“难道你不知道当一个男孩在使用洗手间的时候女孩子是不可以进来的吗!?”我生气地嚷着说。

听到我生气的吼声，她一下子惊呆了，然后“哇”地一声哭了起来。她飞快地关上门向厨房跑去，边哭边向她的父母和我的祖母告状。

大多数的客人其实都听到了我的怒骂声，他们都被逗乐了，可祖母一点都没笑。

She was waiting for me when I left the bathroom. I received the longest, sharpest tongue-lashing of my young life. Grandmother yelled that I was impolite and rude and that I had insulted that nice little girl. The guests watched and winced in absolute silence. So forceful was my grandmother's personality that no one dared stand up for me.

After her harangue was over and I had been dismissed, the party continued, but the atmosphere was much more subdued.

Twenty minutes later, all that changed. Grandmother walked by the bathroom and noticed a torrent of water streaming out from under the door.

She shrieked twice-first in astonishment, then in rage. She flung open the bathroom door and saw that the sink and tub were plugged up and that the faucets were going at full blast.

Everyone knew who the culprit was. The guests quickly formed a protective barricade around me, but Grandmother was so furious that she almost got to me anyway, flailing her arms as if trying to swim over the crowd.

当我从洗手间出来，祖母劈头盖脸地把我骂了一通，骂我没礼貌、少教养、冲撞了那可爱的小女孩。客人们都在静静地看着，我的祖母实在太霸道了，根本没有人敢为我说话。

等她骂完叫我滚开之后，晚会继续进行，但气氛已经大大减弱。

可20分钟之后，一切全都变了。当祖母从洗手间走过的时候，她发现有股水流从门缝里涌出来。

她先是惊异地叫了一声，很快又愤怒地尖叫起来。她猛力地撞开洗手间的门，发现洗手盆和浴缸都被塞子塞住了，水龙头被拧到最大，水正哗啦啦地直流。

每个人都知道是谁搞的鬼，客人们马上在我周围形成了一堵人墙保护我。愤怒的祖母使劲地挥舞着双手，样子就像在人堆里游泳一样。好几次她差点够着我。

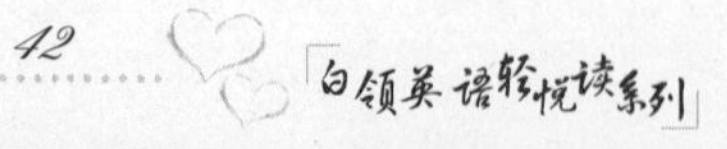

Several strong men eventually moved her away and calmed her down, although she sputtered and fumed for quite a while.

My grandfather took me by the hand and sat me on his lap in a chair near the window. He was a kind and gentle man, full of wisdom and patience. Rarely did he raise his voice to anyone, and never did he argue with his wife or defy her wishes.

He looked at me with much curiosity, not at all angry or upset. "Tell me," he asked, "why did you do it?"

"Well, she yelled at me for nothing," I said earnestly. "Now she's got something to yell about."

Grandfather didn't speak right away. He just sat there, looking at me and smiling.

"Eric," he said at last, "you are my revenge."

最后几个魁梧的男人才把祖母制住，把她拉开让她冷静下来，但她还是气急败坏地嚷了好一阵子。

祖父这时走了过来，牵着我的手到靠窗的一张椅子上坐下，还把我抱到他的膝盖上坐。祖父的性格好，脾气也特别好。他很少提高嗓门和别人说话，也从来没有和祖母吵架，也从来没有违背过祖母的意愿。

他很好奇地打量着我，没有半点生气或烦恼的样子，"告诉我，"他说，"你为什么要这样做呢?"

"是这样的，她先无缘无故地骂了我一顿，"我认真地说，"这回她骂我就有理由了!"

祖父没有马上说话，他只是坐在那儿，笑眯眯地看着我。

最后他终于开口说："艾里克，我的乖孙子，你总算替爷爷出了口气!"

Father in Memory

我记忆中的父亲

Anonymous/佚名

My father was a self-taught mandolin player. He was one of the best string instrument players in our town. He could not read music, but if he heard a tune a few times, he could play it. When he was younger, he was a member of a small country music band. They would play at local dances and on a few occasions would play for the local radio station. He often told us how he had auditioned and earned a position in a band that featured Patsy Cline as their lead singer. He told the family that after he was hired he never went back. Dad was a very religious man. He stated that there was a lot of drinking and cursing the day of his audition and he did not want to be around that type of environment.

我父亲是个自学成才的曼陀林琴手，他是我们镇最优秀的弦乐演奏者之一。他看不懂乐谱，但是如果听几次曲子，他就能演奏出来。当他年轻一点的时候，他是一个小乡村乐队的成员。他们在当地舞厅演奏，有几次还为当地广播电台演奏。他经常告诉我们，自己如何试演，如何在佩茜·克莱恩作为主唱的乐队里占一席之位。他告诉家人，一旦被聘用就永不回头。父亲是一个很严谨的人，他讲述了他试演的那天，很多人在喝酒，咒骂，他不想呆在那种环境里。

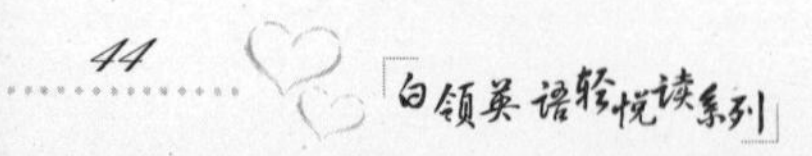

Occasionally, Dad would get out his mandolin and play for the family. We three children: Trisha, Monte and I, George Jr., would often sing along. Songs such as the Tennessee Waltz, Harbor Lights and around Christmas time, the well-known rendition of Silver Bells. "Silver Bells, Silver Bells, its Christmas time in the city" would ring throughout the house. One of Dad's favorite hymns was "The Old Rugged Cross". We learned the words to the hymn when we were very young, and would sing it with Dad when he would play and sing. Another song that was often shared in our house was a song that accompanied the Walt Disney series: Davey Crockett. Dad only had to hear the song twice before he learned it well enough to play it. "Davey, Davey Crockett, King of the Wild Frontier" was a favorite song for the family. He knew we enjoyed the song and the program and would often get out the mandolin after the program was over. I could never get over how he could play the songs so well after only hearing them a few times. I loved to sing, but I never learned how to play the mandolin. This is something I regret to this day.

有时候，父亲会拿出曼陀林，为家人弹奏。我们3个小孩：翠莎、蒙蒂和乔治（也就是我）通常会伴唱。唱的有：《田纳西华尔兹》和《海港之光》，到了圣诞节，就唱脍炙人口的《银铃》："银铃，银铃，城里来了圣诞节。"歌声充满了整个房子。父亲最爱的其中一首赞歌是《古老的十字架》。我们很小的时候就学会歌词了，而且在父亲弹唱的时候，我们也跟着唱。我们经常一起唱的另外一首歌来自沃特·迪斯尼的系列片：《戴维·克罗克特》。父亲只需听两遍就会弹了，"戴维，戴维·克罗克特，荒野边疆的国王。"那是我们家最喜欢的歌曲。他知道我们喜欢那首歌和那个节目，所以每次节目结束后，他就拿出曼陀林弹奏。我永远不能明白他如何能听完几遍后就能把一首曲子弹得那么好。我热爱唱歌，但我没有学会如何弹奏曼陀林，这是我遗憾至今的事情。

Dad loved to play the mandolin for his family he knew we enjoyed singing, and hearing him play. He was like that. If he could give pleasure to others, he would, especially his family. He was always there, sacrificing his time and efforts to see that his family had enough in their life. I had to mature into a man and have children of my own before I realized how much he had sacrificed.

I joined the United States Air Force in January of 1962. Whenever I would come home on leave, I would ask Dad to play the mandolin. Nobody played the mandolin like my father. He could touch your soul with the tones that came out of that old mandolin. He seemed to shine when he was playing. You could see his pride in his ability to play so well for his family.

父亲喜欢为家人弹奏曼陀林，他知道我们喜欢唱歌，喜欢听他弹奏。他就是那样，如果他能把快乐奉献给别人，他从不吝啬，尤其是对他的家人。他总是那样，牺牲自己的时间和精力让家人生活得满足。父亲的这种付出是只有当我长大成人，而且是有了自己的孩子后才能体会到的。

我在 1962 年 1 月加入了美国空军。每当我休假回家，我都请求父亲弹奏曼陀林。没有人弹奏曼陀林能达到像我父亲那样的境界，他在那古老的曼陀林上抚出的旋律能够触及你的灵魂。他弹奏的时候，身上似乎能发出四射的光芒。你可以看出，父亲为能给家人弹奏出如此美妙的旋律，他是多么地自豪。

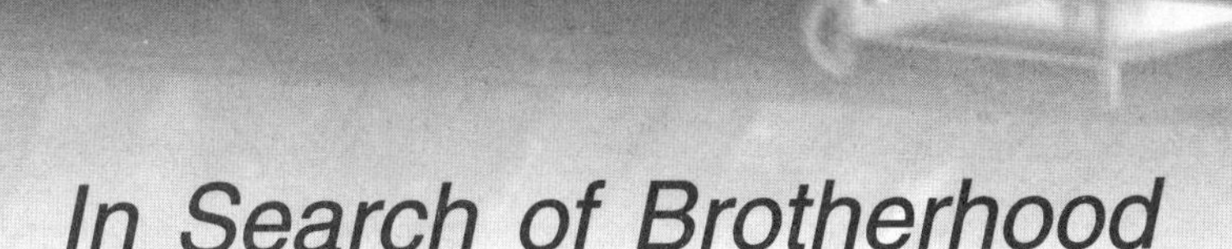

In Search of Brotherhood

重拾旧谊

Anonymous/佚名

I am not really sure when our boundaries went up. Men tend to build walls quietly, without warning. All I know is that when I looked up, we weren't talking anymore. Somehow we had become like strangers.

This rift — a simple misunderstanding magnified by male ego — didn't happen overnight. Men aren't like some women I know; we don't announce that we are cutting each other off. Instead, we just slowly starve the relationship of anything substantive until it fades away.

Me and my buddy had let our friendship evaporate to a point where we hadn't spoken in almost two years. Then one morning my mother called me at work and shared something she'd heard about him. "You know, his wife is sick with cancer." she said.

I had to close my office door. I don't cry often, but the news broke me down. I thought of his wedding day four years ago and a picture I snapped of him beaming at me as he wrapped his bride in his arms. I remember telling my wife that I'd never seen him so happy, so sure about something.

As it hit me that he now faced the possibility of losing his love, a deep sense of shame came over me. I wondered how he was coping and who was helping him through this crisis. I thought how devastated I'd be if my own wife were suffering. And I wondered whether he and I could ever be tight again.

We had always been like family, sharing an unusual history that dated back to the turn of the century when our great-grandparents were pals growing up in a small town not far from Nashville. Both our families migrated north to Detroit for better-paying jobs, and remained close through the generations.

When I was born 36 years ago, he was among my first playmates. As we grew older, we became what we called true boys — real aces, spending most of our time together running the streets, hanging at bars and clubs, watching games and chasing women. Our friendship came so easily that we took it for granted, and when it began to unravel, neither of us had a clue how to mend it.

很难说清从什么时候我们之间开始渐渐疏远的。男人间的隔阂总是产生于无声无息之间，事先没有任何预兆。直到有一天蓦然回首时才发现我们不再促膝倾谈，疏远得有些形同陌路了。

这种隔阂并不会在一夜之间突然形成，它是男人的自我中心在作祟。男人不会像我认识的一些女人一样宣称断绝彼此的往来，他们会渐渐地淡化彼此的关系，直到这感情慢慢地烟消云散。

我与朋友的关系就处在这样的淡却中，两年来，我们没说过一句话。直到一天早上，在上班的时候母亲打来一个电话，告诉我她刚刚知道的关于他的消息："他的妻子患了癌症。"

我关上了房门，眼泪流了下来，我很少哭，但这消息让我很心痛。4年前参加他婚礼的情景还历历在目，当时他把新娘拥在怀中，对着我的镜头灿烂地笑。我还记得后来对我妻子说，我从没见过他那么义无反顾、那么幸福。

如今，想到他可能会由此失去爱人，我忽然觉得很惭愧。他该如何面对，又有谁会帮他共渡难关呢？如果自己处在这样的境况，该是多么绝望！我们能不能重拾旧谊呢？我不由问自己。

我们曾经就像一家人，两家的渊源可追溯到本世纪之初，我们的曾祖父母是同在田纳西州纳什维尔市不远的小镇上一起长大的伙伴。两家后来又都为了寻求更好的工作向北迁移到了底特律，大家仍然保持密切的联系，几代世交。

从我出生到现在我36岁，他一直是我从小玩到大的亲密伙伴。我们共同成长，一起度过躁动的青春时光，成天在街头闲逛，流连在酒吧舞台，为球赛呐喊助威，一起追风逐蝶，还自认为是少年风范，男儿本色。我们的友谊仿佛与生俱来，自然得让我们觉得理所当然，以至当裂缝悄然出现，我们竟都不知该如何修补。

The Small White Envelope

白色小信封

Anonymous/佚名

It's just a small, white envelope stuck among the branches of our Christmas tree. No name, no identification, no inscription. It has peeked through the branches of our tree for the past 10 years or so.

It all began because my husband Mike hated Christmas. He didn't hate the true meaning of Christmas, but the commercial aspects of it; overspending, the frantic running around at the last minute to get a tie for Uncle Harry and the dusting powder for Grandma and the gifts given in desperation because you couldn't think of anything else.

Knowing he felt this way, I decided one year to bypass the usual shirts, sweaters, ties and so forth. I reached for something special just for Mike. The inspiration came in an unusual way.

我家的圣诞树上挂着一张小小的白色信封。上面既没有收信人的名字和寄信人的签名，也没有任何提示。它挂在我家的圣诞树上已经10多年了。

一切都因丈夫迈克对圣诞的憎恨而起。他并不憎恨圣诞节本身的意义，但他讨厌圣诞被商业化了。人们大把大把地花钱；在平安夜的最后一分钟，围着圈不顾一切地跑去为哈里大叔抢些彩带，为外祖母抢些彩粉；疯狂地瓜分礼物，把一切都抛在脑后。

正是因为知道他的这种感受，于是有一年我决定打破常规（平时都送些衬衣、毛衣或是领带等礼物）。我为迈克准备了一些特别的东西。灵感是有来历的。

Our son Kevin, who was 12 that year, was wrestling at the junior level at the school he attended and shortly before Christmas, there was a non-league match against a team sponsored by an inner-city church, mostly black.

These youngsters, dressed in sneakers so ragged that shoestrings seemed to be the only thing holding them together, presented a sharp contrast to our boys in their spiffy blue and gold uniforms and sparkling new wrestling shoes.

As the match began, I was alarmed to see that the other team was wrestling without headgear, a kind of light helmet designed to protect a wrestler's ears.

It was a luxury the ragtag team obviously could not afford. Well, we ended up walloping them. We took every weight class. And as each of their boys got up from the mat, he swaggered around in his tatters with false bravado, a kind of street pride that couldn't acknowledge defeat.

那年我们的儿子凯文12岁，在学校摔跤队的初级班里接受训练。圣诞节前夕，学校安排了一场非联赛的比赛，对手是本市教会资助的一只队伍，他们大部分队员都是黑人。

这些小伙子们穿着破烂不堪的运动鞋，唯一能够绑在脚上的仿佛只有那条鞋带。而与之形成鲜明对比的是我们的孩子，他们身披金蓝相间的制服，脚蹬崭新的摔跤鞋，显得分外耀眼。

比赛开始了，我惊异地发现对方选手在摔跤的时候没有带专业头盔，只有一种好像质地很薄的帽子保护着选手的耳朵。

对贫民队来说买一顶头盔显然是一种奢侈。毫无疑问我们以绝对的优势获胜，并取得了每个级别的冠军。比赛结束了，他们队的每个男孩从地毯上爬起来，在溃败的失意中昂首阔步装出一副获胜的样子，流露出像街头少年般不愿认输的傲慢。

Mike, seated beside me, shook his head sadly, "I wish just one of them could have won," he said. "They have a lot of potential, but losing like this could take the heart right out of them."

Mike loved kids — all kids — and he knew them, having coached little league football, baseball and lacrosse. That's when the idea for his present came.

That afternoon, I went to a local sporting goods store and bought an assortment of wrestling headgear and shoes and sent them anonymously to the inner-city church.

On Christmas Eve, I placed the envelope on the tree, the note inside telling Mike what I had done and that this was his gift from me. His smile was the brightest thing about Christmas that year and in succeeding years.

For each Christmas, I followed the tradition, one year sending a group of mentally handicapped youngsters to a hockey game, another year a check to a pair of elderly brothers whose home had burned to the ground the week before Christmas, and on and on.

坐在我身旁的迈克伤心地摇摇头说道："我真希望他们其中一个可以赢。他们很有潜力，但是就这样输掉了比赛就等于输掉了他们的信心。"

迈克爱孩子——所有的孩子。他曾带过小型的联赛橄榄球队、棒球队和长曲棍球队，所以他了解他们。而我的灵感也由此而发。

当天下午，我就到本地的一家运动用品商店买了摔跤专用的头盔和鞋子，并以匿名的形式把礼物送到了本市的教会。

那个圣诞夜，我把一个信封挂在圣诞树上，里面写着我做的事情，并告诉迈克这是我送给他的礼物。他的笑容是那年圣诞节最明亮的饰物，多少年来那笑容还一直延续着。

每年的圣诞节，我都沿袭了这个传统。我曾送给一群智障儿童一副曲棍球，也曾送给一对年老的兄弟一张支票，因为圣诞节的前一个星期大火烧毁了他们的房子，等等，等等。

Not "Just a Mom"

不仅仅是位母亲

Anonymous/佚名

A woman named Emily renewing her driver's license at the County Clerk's office was asked by the woman recorder to state her occupation. She hesitated, uncertain how to classify herself. "What I mean is," explained the recorder, "do you have a job, or are you just a..."

"Of course I have a job," snapped Emily. "I'm a mother."

"We don't list 'mother' as an occupation 'Housewife' covers it," said the recorder emphatically.

I forgot all about her story until one day I found myself in the same situation, this time at our own Town Hall. The Clerk was obviously a career woman, poised, efficient, and possessed of a high sounding title like, "Official Interrogator" or "Town Registrar". "What is your occupation?" she probed.

一位名叫埃米莉的妇女在县办事处给驾驶执照续期时，一名女记录员问及她的职业。她犹豫了一下，不敢肯定应如何将自己归类。"我意思是说你有没有工作，"那名记录员解释说，"还是说你只不过是一名……"

"我当然有工作，"埃米莉马上回答，"我是一名母亲。"

"我们这里不把'母亲'看成是一个职业……'家庭主妇'就可以了。"那名记录员断然回答。

这个故事听后，我就忘了。直到有一天在市政厅，我也遇到了同样的情况。很显然，那名办事员是位职业女性，自信、有能力，并有着一个类似"官方讯问员"或"镇登记员"之类很堂皇的头衔。"你的职业?"她问道。

What made me say it, I do not know The words simply popped out. "I'm a Research Associate in the field of Child Development and Human Relations."

The clerk paused, ballpoint pen frozen in midair, and looked up as though she had not heard right.

I repeated the title slowly, emphasizing the most significant words. Then I stared with wonder as my pronouncement was written in bold, black ink on the official questionnaire.

"Might I ask," said the clerk with new interest, "just what you do in your field?"

Coolly, without any trace of fluster in my voice, I heard myself reply, "I have a continuing program of research, (what mother doesn't), in the laboratory and in the field, (normally I would have said indoors and out). I'm working for my Masters, (the whole darned family), and already have four credits, (all daughters). Of course, the job is one of the most demanding in the humanities, (any mother care to disagree?) and I often work 14 hours a day, (24 is more like it). But the job is more challenging than most run-of-the-mill careers and the rewards are more of a satisfaction rather than just money."

至今我也不知道，当时是什么因素作怪，我脱口而出："我是儿童发育和人类关系研究员。"

那名办事员愣住了，拿着圆珠笔的手也不动了。她抬头看着我，好像没有听清楚我说什么似的。

我慢慢地把我的职业再重复一遍，在说到重要的词时还加重语气。然后，我惊奇地看着我的话被粗黑的笔记录在官方的问卷上。

"我能不能问一下，"这名办事员好奇地问，"你在这个领域具体做什么？"

我非常镇定地答道："我有一个不间断的研究项目（哪位母亲不是这样呢?），工作地点包括实验室和现场（通常我会说室内和户外）。我在为我的学位努力（就是我们一家人），而且已经有了4个学分（全部是女儿）。当然，我的工作是人类要求最高的工作之一（有哪位母亲会反对吗?）我通常一天工作14小时（24小时更为准确）。但这项工作比大部分普通工作都具有挑战性，而它通常带来的回报不是金钱，更多的是满足感。"

There was an increasing note of respect in the clerk's voice as she completed the form, stood up, and personally ushered me to the door.

As I drove into our driveway, buoyed up by my glamorous new career, I was greeted by my lab assistants — ages 13, 7, and 3. Upstairs I could hear our new experimental model, (a 6-month-old baby), in the child-development program, testing out a new vocal pattern.

I felt triumphant! I had scored a beat on bureaucracy! And I had gone on the official records as someone more distinguished and indispensable to mankind than "just another mother".

Motherhood What a glorious career! Especially when there's a title on the door.

那名办事员在填完表格后，站起来，亲自把我送到门口。在这个过程中，她说话时流露出一股敬意。

我回到家，把车停在家门前的车道时，还对自己响亮的头衔觉得飘飘然。我那三名年龄分别为13岁、7岁、3岁的实验室助手正在等着我，从楼上传来我们的新实验模特儿（6个月大的婴儿）的声音，她正放开嗓门，测试着新的声音模式。

我感到欢欣鼓舞！我竟然打败了官僚机构！如今，在官方的纪录上，我成了人类超群出众、不可或缺的人物，而不仅仅是一位母亲。

母亲，多么荣耀的一项职业！尤其是当她还有一个动听的头衔。

My Father

我的父亲

Anonymous/佚名

The first memory I have of him — of anything, really — is his strength. It was in the late afternoon in a house under construction near ours. The unfinished wood floor had large, terrifying holes whose yawning darkness I knew led to nowhere good. His powerful hands, then age 33, wrapped all the way around my tiny arms, then age 4, and easily swung me up to his shoulders to command all I surveyed.

The relationship between a son and his father changes over time. It may grow and flourish in mutual maturity. It may sour in resented dependence or independence. With many children living in single-parent homes today, it may not even exist.

我对他——实际上是对所有事的最初记忆，就是他的力量。那是一个下午的晚些时候，在一所靠近我家的正在修建的房子里，尚未完工的木地板上有一个个巨大的可怕的洞，那些张着大口的黑洞在我看来是通向不祥之处的。时年33岁的爸爸用他那强壮有力的双手一把握住我的小胳膊，当时我才4岁，然后轻而易举地把我甩上他的肩头，让我把一切都尽收眼底。

父子间的关系是随着岁月的流逝而变化的，它会在彼此成熟的过程中成长兴盛，也会在令人不快的依赖或独立的关系中产生不和。而今许多孩子生活在单亲家庭中，这种关系可能根本不存在。

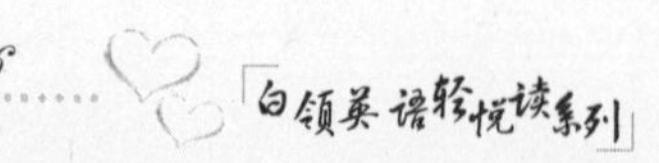

But to a little boy right after World War II, a father seemed a god with strange strengths and uncanny powers enabling him to do and know things that no mortal could do or know. Amazing things, like putting a bicycle chain back on, just like that. Or building a hamster cage. Or guiding a jigsaw so it forms the letter F; I learned the alphabet that way in those pre-television days.

There were, of course, rules to learn. First came the handshake. None of those fishylittle finger grips, but a good firm squeeze accompanied by an equally strong gaze into the other's eyes. "The first thing anyone knows about you is your handshake," he would say. And we'd practice it each night on his return from work, the serious toddler in the battered Cleveland Indian's cap running up to the giant father to shake hands again and again until it was firm enough.

As time passed, there were other rules to learn. "Always do your best." "Do it now." "Never lie!" And most importantly, "You can do whatever you have to do." By my teens, he wasn't telling me what to do anymore, which was scary and heady at the same time. He provided perspective, not telling me what was around the great corner of life but letting me know there was a lot more than just today and the next, which I hadn't thought of.

然而，对于一个生活在第二次世界大战刚刚结束时期的小男孩来说，父亲就像神，他拥有神奇的力量和神秘的能力，他无所不能，无所不知。那些奇妙的事儿有上自行车链条，或是制作一个仓鼠笼子，或是教我玩拼图玩具，拼出个字母“F”来。在那个电视机还未诞生的年代，我便是通过这种方法学会了字母表的。

当然，还得学些做人的道理。首先是握手。这可不是指那种冷冰冰的手指相握，而是一种非常坚定有力的紧握，并同样坚定有力地注视对方的眼睛。老爸常说：“人们认识你首先是通过同你握手。”每晚他下班回家时，我们便练习握手。年幼的我，戴着顶破克利夫兰印第安帽，一本正经地跌跌撞撞地跑向巨人般的父亲，开始我们的握手。一次又一次，直到握得坚定、有力。

随着时间的流逝，还有许多其他的道理要学。比如：“始终尽力而为”，“从现在做起”，“永不撒谎”，以及最重要的一条：“凡是你必须做的事你都能做到”。当我十几岁时，老爸不再叫我做这做那，这既令人害怕又令人兴奋。他教给我判断事物的方法。他不是告诉我，在人生的重大转折点上将发生些什么，而是让我明白，除了今天和明天，还有很长的路要走，这一点我是从未考虑过的。

One day, I realize now, there was a change. I wasn't trying to please him so much as I was trying to impress him. I never asked him to come to my football games. He had a high-pressure career, and it meant driving through most of Friday night. But for all the big games, when I looked over at the sideline, there was that familiar fedora. And by God, did the opposing team captain ever get a firm handshake and a gaze he would remember.

Then, a school fact contradicted something he said. Impossible that he could be wrong, but there it was in the book. These accumulated over time, along with personal experiences, to buttress my own developing sense of values. And I could tell we had each taken our own, perfectly normal paths.

I began to see, too, his blind spots, his prejudices and his weaknesses. I never threw these up at him. He hadn't to me, and, anyway, he seemed to need protection. I stopped asking his advice; the experiences he drew from no longer seemed relevant to the decisions I had to make.

有一天，事情发生了变化，这是我现在才意识到的。我不再那么迫切地想要取悦于老爸，而是迫切地想要给他留下深刻的印象。我从未请他来看我的橄榄球赛。他工作压力很大，这意味着每个星期五要拼命干大半夜。但每次大型比赛，当我抬头环视看台时，那顶熟悉的软呢帽总在那儿。并且感谢上帝，对方队长总能得到一次让他铭记于心的握手——坚定而有力，伴以同样坚定的注视。

后来，在学校学到的一个事实否定了老爸说过的某些东西。他不可能会错的，可书上却是这样写的。诸如此类的事日积月累，加上我的个人阅历，支持了我逐渐成形的价值观。我可以这么说：我俩开始各走各的阳关道了。

与此同时，我还开始发现他对某些事的无知，他的偏见，他的弱点。我从未在他面前提起这些，他也从未在我面前说起，而且，不管怎么说，他看起来需要保护了。我不再向他征求意见；他的那些经验也似乎同我要作出的决定不再相干。

He volunteered advice for a while. But then, in more recent years, politics and issues gave way to talk of empty errands and, always, to ailments.

From his bed, he showed me the many sores and scars on his misshapen body and all the bottles for medicine. “Sometimes,” he confided, “I would just like to lie down and go to sleep and not wake up.”

After much thought and practice (“You can do whatever you have to do.”), one night last winter, I sat down by his bed and remembered for an instant those terrifying dark holes in another house 35 years before. I told my father how much I loved him. I described all the things people were doing for him. But, I said, he kept eating poorly, hiding in his room and violating the doctor's orders. No amount of love could make someone else care about life, I said; it was a two-way street. He wasn't doing his best. The decision was his.

老爸当了一段时间的“自愿顾问”，但后来，特别是近几年里，他谈话中的政治与国家大事让位给了空洞的使命与疾病。

躺在床上，他给我看他那被岁月扭曲了的躯体上的疤痕，以及他所有的药瓶儿。他倾诉着：“有时我真想躺下睡一觉，永远不再醒来。”

通过深思熟虑与亲身体验（“凡是你必须做的事你都能做到”），去年冬天的一个夜晚，我坐在老爸床边，忽然想起35年前那另一栋房子里可怕的黑洞。我告诉老爸我有多爱他。我向他讲述了人们为他所做的一切。而我又说，他总是吃得太少，躲在房间里，还不听医生的劝告。我说，再多的爱也不能使一个人自己去热爱生命：这是一条双行道，而他并没有尽力，一切都取决于他自己。

He said he knew how hard my words had been to say and how proud he was of me. “I had the best teacher,” I said. “You can do whatever you have to do.” He smiled a little. And we shook hands, firmly, for the last time.

Several days later, at about 4 A. M. , my mother heard Dad shuffling about their dark room. “I have some things I have to do,” he said. He paid a bundle of bills. He composed for my mother a long list of legal and financial what-to-do’s “in case of emergency.” And he wrote me a note.

Then he walked back to his bed and laid himself down. He went to sleep, naturally. And he did not wake up.

他说他明白要我说出这些话多不容易，他是多么为我自豪。“我有位最好的老师，”我说，“凡是你必须做的事你都能做到。”他微微一笑，之后我们握手，那是一次坚定的握手，也是最后的一次。

几天后，大约凌晨 4 点，母亲听到父亲拖着脚步在他们漆黑的房间里走来走去。他说：“有些事我必须得做。”他支付了一摞账单，给母亲留了张长长的条子，上面列有法律及经济上该做的事，“以防不测”。接着他留了封短信给我。

然后，他走回自己的床边，躺下。他睡了，十分安详，再也没有醒来。

Anonymous/佚名

She had been shopping with her Mom in Wal-Mart. She must have been 6 years old, this beautiful brown haired, freckle-faced image of innocence. It was pouring outside. The kind of rain that gushes over the top of rain gutters, so much in a hurry to hit the Earth it has no time to flow down the spout.

We all stood there under the awning and just inside the door of the Wal-Mart. We waited, some patiently, others irritated because nature messed up their hurried day. I am always mesmerized by rainfall. I get lost in the sound and sight of the heavens washing away the dirt and dust of the world. Memories of running, splashing so carefree as a child come pouring in as a welcome reprieve from the worries of my day.

Her voice was so sweet as it broke the hypnotic trance we were all caught in. "Mom, let's run through the rain," she said.

"What?" Mom asked.

"Let's run through the rain!" She repeated.

她和妈妈刚在沃尔玛超市购完物。这个天真的小女孩应该6岁大了，头发是美丽的棕色，脸上有雀斑。外面下着倾盆大雨。雨水溢满了檐槽，迫不及待地涌向大地，来不及排走。

我们都站在沃尔玛超市门口的遮篷下。大家在等待，有的人很耐心，也有人烦躁，因为老天在给他们本已忙碌的一天添乱。雨天总引起我的遐思。我出神地听着、看着老天洗刷冲走这世界的污垢和尘埃，孩时无忧无虑地在雨中奔跑玩水的记忆汹涌而至，暂时缓解了我这一天的焦虑。

小女孩甜美的声音打破了这令人昏昏欲睡的气氛，“妈妈，我们在雨里跑吧，”她说。

“什么?”母亲问。

“我们在雨里跑吧，”她重复。

“No, honey. We'll wait until it slows down a bit,” Mom replied.

This young child waited about another minute and repeated: “Mom, let's run through the rain.”

“We'll get soaked if we do,” Mom said.

"No, we won't, Mom. That's not what you said this morning," the young girl said as she tugged at her Mom's arm.

"This morning? When did I say we could run through the rain and not get wet?"

"Don't you remember? When you were talking to Daddy about his cancer, you said, 'If God can get us through this, he can get us through anything!'"

The entire crowd stopped dead silent. I swear you couldn't hear anything but the rain. We all stood silently. No one came or left in the next few minutes. Mom paused and thought for a moment about what she would say.

Now some would laugh it off and scold her for being silly. Some might even ignore what was said. But this was a moment of affirmation in a young child's life. Time when innocent trust can be nurtured so that it will bloom into faith. "Honey, you are absolutely right. Let's run through the rain. If get wet, well maybe we just needed washing," Mom said. Then off they ran.

We all stood watching, smiling and laughing as they darted past the cars and. They held their shopping bags over their heads just in case. They got soaked. But they were followed by a few who screamed and laughed like children all the way to their cars. And yes, I did. I ran. I got wet. I needed washing. Circumstances or people can take away your material possessions, they can take away your money, and they can take away your health. But no one can ever take away your precious memories. So, don't forget to make time and take the opportunities to make memories every day!

To everything there is a season and a time to every purpose under heaven. I hope you still take the time to run through the rain.

“不，亲爱的，我们等雨小一点再走，”母亲回答说。

过了一会儿小女孩又说：“妈妈，我们跑出去吧。”

“这样的话我们会湿透的，”母亲说。

“不会的，妈妈。你今天早上不是这样说的。”小女孩一边说一边拉着母亲的手。

“今天早上？我什么时候说过我们淋雨不会湿啊？”

“你不记得了吗？你和爸爸谈他的癌症时，你不是说‘如果上帝让我们闯过这一关，那我们就没有什么过不去的。’”

人群一片寂静。我发誓，除了雨声，你什么都听不到。我们都静静地站着。接下来的几分钟没有一个人走动。母亲停了一下，在想着应该说些什么。

有人也许会对此一笑了之，或者责备这孩子的不懂事，有人甚至不把她的话放在心上。但这却是一个小孩子一生中需要被肯定的时候。若受到鼓舞，此时孩子单纯的信任就会发展成为坚定的信念。“亲爱的，你说得对，我们跑过去吧。如果淋湿了，那也许是因为我们的确需要冲洗一下了，”母亲说。然后她们就冲出去了。

我们站在那里，笑着看她们飞快地跑过停着的汽车。他们把购物袋高举过头想挡挡雨，但还是湿透了。好几个人像孩子般尖叫着，大笑着，也跟着冲了出去，奔向自己的车子。当然，我也这样做了，跑了出去，淋湿了。我也需要接受洗礼。环境或其他人可以夺去你的物质财富，抢走你的金钱，带走你的健康，但没有人可以带走你珍贵的回忆。因此，记得要抓紧时间，抓住机会每天都给自己留下一些回忆吧！

世间万物皆有自己的季节，做任何事情也有一个恰当的时机。希望你有机会在雨中狂奔一回。

Don't Stop
别停下，继续弹

Anonymous/佚名

Wishing to encourage her young son's progress on the piano, a mother took her boy to a Paderewski concert. After they were seated, the mother spotted a friend in the audience and walked down the aisle to greet her.

Seizing the opportunity to explore the wonders of the concert hall, the little boy rose and eventually explored his way through a door marked "NO ADMITTANCE". When the house lights dimmed and the concert was about to begin, the mother returned to her seat and discovered that the child was missing.

Suddenly, the curtains parted and spotlights focused on the impressive Steinway on stage. In horror, the mother saw her little boy sitting at the key-board, innocently picking out Twinkle, Twinkle Little Star.

At that moment, the great piano master made his entrance, quickly moved to the piano, and whispered in the boy's ear, "Don't quit. Keep playing."

Then leaning over, Paderewski reached down with his left hand and began filling in a bass part. Soon his right arm reached around to the other side of the child and he added a running obbligato. Together, the old master and the young novice transformed a frightening situation into a wonderfully creative experience. The audience was mesmerized.

That's the way it is in life. What we can accomplish on our own is hardly noteworthy. We try our best, but the results aren't exactly graceful flowing

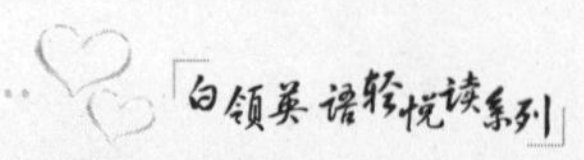

music. But when we trust in the hands of a Greater Power, our life's work truly can be beautiful.

Next time you set out to accomplish great feats, listen carefully. You can hear the voice of the Master, whispering in your ear, "Don't quit. Keep playing."

为了让儿子能在钢琴方面有长足的进步，一位母亲带着儿子去听帕德瑞夫斯基的音乐会。待他们坐定之后，那位母亲看到一位熟人，就穿过走道过去跟朋友打招呼。

小男孩好不容易有机会欣赏音乐厅的宏伟，他站了起来，并慢慢地摸索到了一扇门旁边，上面写着“禁止入内”。大厅里的灯暗了下来，音乐会马上就要开始了。那位母亲回到座位，却发现自己的孩子不见了。

这时候，幕布徐徐拉开，大厅里的聚光灯都集中到了舞台上的士坦威钢琴上。而让母亲吃惊的是，她的儿子竟然坐在钢琴面前，自顾自地弹着“闪烁，闪烁，小星星”。

这时候，著名的钢琴大师走上台，并且迅速地走到钢琴旁边，并在男孩的耳边轻声说道：“孩子，别停下，继续弹。”

帕德瑞夫斯基俯下身去，用左手在键盘上弹奏低音部分。然后，他的右手绕过男孩的身后，弹奏出优美的伴奏。这位年长的钢琴大师和年幼的初学者一起，将原本紧张的气氛变成了一种全新的体验。全场的观众都听得入迷了。

其实，生活也是如此。我们所取得的成就不一定要多么显著。我们尽力了，结果却不一定能演奏出优美流畅的音乐。但是，如果我们相信大师的力量，我们的生活就会变得非常美丽。

当你准备伟大作品的时候，仔细地侧耳倾听，你会听到大师的声音，在你耳边轻声说道：“别停下，继续弹！”

Home, Sweet Home 家，甜蜜的家

John. H. Payne / 约翰·H·佩恩

(1) Mid pleasures and palaces though we may roam,

虽然我们也会沉迷于欢乐与奢靡中，

Be it ever so humble, there's no place like home!

无论家是多么简陋，没有地方比得上它！

A charm from the skies seems to hallow us there,

好似从空而降的魔力，使我们在家觉得圣洁，

Which seek through the world, is ne'er met with elsewhere,

就是找遍全世界，也找不到像这样的地方，

Home! Home! Sweet, sweet Home!

家啊！家啊！甜蜜的家啊！

There's no place like Home! There's no place like Home!

没有地方比得上家！没有地方比得上家！

(2) I gaze on the moon as I tread the drear wild,
每当我漫步荒野凝视明月，

And feel that my mother now thinks of her child,
便想起母亲正惦念着她的孩子，

As she looks on that moon from our own cottage door,
当她从茅舍门口遥望明月时，

Through the woodbine，whose fragrance shall cheer me no more.
穿过忍冬树丛，浓郁树香再也不能安慰我的心灵。

Home! Home! Sweet, sweet Home!
家啊！家啊！甜蜜的家啊！

There's no place like Home! There's no place like Home!
没有地方比得上家！没有地方比得上家！

(3) An exile from home, splendor dazzles in vain;
对离乡背井的游子，再华丽的光辉，也是徒然闪烁；

Oh，give me my lowly thatch'd cottage again!
一栋矮檐茅舍！

The birds singing gaily, that came at my call —
一呼即来的鸟儿正在欢唱——

Give me them, and the peace of mind, dearer than all!
赐给我它们——还有心灵的平静，这些胜过一切！

Home! Home! Sweet, sweet Home!
家啊！家啊！甜蜜的家啊！

There's no place like Home! There's no place like Home!
没有地方比得上家！没有地方比得上家！

Mother in Their Eyes

名人眼中的母亲

Anonymous/佚名

All that I am or ever hope to be, I owe to my angel Mother. I remember my mother's prayers and they have always followed me. They have clung to me all my life.

——*Abraham Lincoln* (1809—1865)

无论我现在怎么样，还是希望以后会怎么样，都应当归功于我天使一般的母亲。我记得母亲的那些祷告，它们一直伴随着我，而且已经陪伴了我一生。

——亚伯拉罕·林肯

My mother was the most beautiful woman I ever saw. All I am I owe to my mother. I attribute all my success in life to the moral, intellectual and physical education I received from her.

——*George Washington* (1732—1799)

我的母亲是我见过的最漂亮的女人。我所有的一切都归功于我的母亲。我一生中所有的成就都归功于我从她那儿得到的德、智、体的教育。

——乔治·华盛顿

There never was a woman like her. She was gentle as a dove and brave as a lioness… The memory of my mother and her teachings were, after all, the only capital I had to start life with, and on that capital I have made my way.

——*Andrew Jackson* (1767—1845)

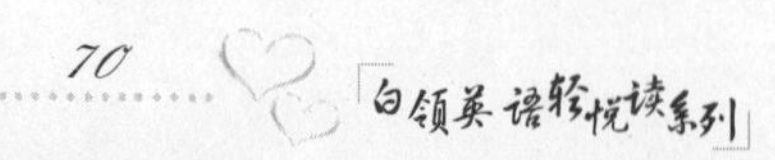

从来没有一个女人像她那样。她非常温柔，就像一只鸽子；她也很勇敢，就像一头母狮……毕竟，对母亲的记忆和她的教诲是我人生起步的唯一资本，并奠定了我的人生之路。

——安德鲁·杰克逊

A good mother is worth a hundred schoolmaster.

——*George Herbert*（1593—1633）

一位好母亲抵得上一百个教师。

——乔治·赫伯特

Youth fades; love droops; the leaves of friendship fall. A mother's secret hope outlives them all.

——*Oliver Wendell Holmes*（1809—1894）

青春会逝去；爱情会枯萎；友谊的绿叶也会凋零。而一个母亲内心的希望比它们都要长久。

——奥利弗·温戴尔·荷马

God could not be everywhere and therefore he made mothers.

——*Jewish proverb*

上帝不能无处不在，因此他创造了母亲。

——犹太谚语

The heart of a mother is a deep abyss at the bottom of which you will always find forgiveness.

——*Balzac*（1799—1850）

母亲的心是一个深渊，在它的最深处你总会得到宽恕。

——巴尔扎克

The most important thing a father can do for his children is to love their mother.

——*Author Unknown*

父亲能够为孩子所做的最重要的事就是爱他们的母亲。

——无名氏

In all my efforts to learn to read, my mother shared fully my ambition and sympathized with me and aided me in every way she could. If I have done anything in life worth attention, I feel sure that I inherited the disposition from my mother.

——*Booker T. Washington* (1881—1915)

在我努力学习阅读的过程中，母亲一直分享着我的抱负、充分理解我，尽她所能帮助我。如果我一生中做了什么值得人们注意的事情，那一定是因为我继承了她的气质。

——布克.T. 华盛顿

It seems to me that my mother was the most splendid woman I ever knew… I have met a lot of people knocking around the world since, but I have never met a more thoroughly refined woman than my mother. If I have amounted to anything, it will be due to her.

——*Charles Chaplin* (1889—1977)

对我而言，我的母亲似乎是我认识的最了不起的女人……我遇见太多太多的世人，可是从未遇上像我母亲那般优雅的女人。如果我有所成就的话，这要归功于她。

——查尔斯·卓别林

Unconditional Mother's Love

无条件的母爱

Anonymous/佚名

I was a rotten teenager. Not a common spoiled, know-it-all, not-going-to-clean-my room, and self-conscious teenager. No, I was sharp-tongued and eager to control others. I told lies. And I realized at an early age that I could make things go my way with just a few small changes. The writers for today's hottest soap opera could not have created a worse character than me.

For the most part, and on the outside, I was a good kid, a giggly tomboy who liked to play sports and who was good at competition. This is probably why most people forgave me for my bad behavior towards people I felt to be of value.

Since I was clever enough to get some people to give in to me, I don't know how long it took me to realize how I was hurting so many others. Not only did I succeed in pushing away many of my closest friends by trying to control them; I also managed to destroy, time and time again, the most precious relationship in my life: my relationship with my mother.

Even today, almost 10 years since the birth of the new me, my former behavior astonishes me each time I reach into my memories. Hurtful words that cut and stung the people I cared most about. Acts of confusion and anger that seemed to rule my every move — all to make sure that things went my way.

My mother, who gave birth to me at age 38 against her doctor's wishes, would cry to me, "I waited so long for you, please don't push me away. I want to help you!"

I would reply sharply, "I didn't ask for you! I never wanted you to care about me! Leave me alone and forget I ever lived!"

My mother began to believe I really meant it. My actions proved that.

I was mean and eager to control, trying to get my way at any cost. Like many young girls in high school, the boys whom I knew were impossible were always the first ones I had to date. I would get out of the house without my mother's knowing very late at night just to prove I could do it. I would readily tell complex lies without hesitation. I would also try to find any way to draw attention to myself while at the same time trying to be invisible.

I had been heavy into drugs during that period of my life, taking mind-changing pills and smoking things that changed my personality. That accounted for the terrible, sharp words that came flying from my mouth. However, that was not the case. My only addiction was hatred; my only pleasure was to make people feel pain.

But then I asked myself why. Why the need to hurt? And why the people I cared about the most? Why the need for all the lies? Why the attacks on my mother? I would drive myself mad with all the whys until one day, I couldn't stand it any longer and jump from a car moving at 80 miles per hour.

Lying awake the following night at the hospital, I came to realize that I didn't want to die.

And I did not want to inflict any more pain on people to cover up what I was truly trying to hide myself: self-hatred. Self-hatred inflicted on everyone else.

I saw my mother's pained face for the first time in years — warm, tired brown eyes filled with nothing but thanks for her daughter's rebirth of life and love for the child she waited 38 years to bear.

My first experience with unconditional love. What a powerful feeling.

Despite all the lies I had told her, she still loved me. I cried on her lap for hours one afternoon and asked why she still loved me after all the horrible things I did to her. She just looked down at me, brushed the hair out of my face and said frankly, "I don't know."

A kind of smile came out of her tears as the lines in her tested face told me all that I needed to know. I was her daughter, but more important, she was my mother. Not every rotten child is so lucky. Not every mother can be pushed to the limits time and time again, and come back with feelings of love.

Unconditional love is the most precious gift we can give. Being forgiven for the past is the most precious gift we can receive. I dare not say we could experience this pure love twice in one lifetime.

I was one of the lucky ones. I know that. I want to extend the gift my mother gave me to all the "rotten teenagers" in the world who are confused.

It's okay to feel pain, to need help, to feel love — just feel it without hiding. Come out from under the hard and protective covers, and take a breath of life.

我曾是个堕落的小丫头，不是一般地被宠坏，自以为是、不愿意打扫房间且自我意识强的那种。不，我不是那样的。我说话刻薄，控制别人的欲望强，又说谎。很早我就知道只要做些小小的变通，就可以随心所欲地操纵局面。就是现在最热门的肥皂剧作家也没能力塑造出比我更坏的角色。

多数时候，从表面上看，我是个好孩子，一个嘻嘻哈哈的假小子，喜欢体育运动，比赛常拿名次。或许正因为如此，尽管我对那些有身份的人任性胡来，他们中大多数人还是原谅了我。

我很精明，总有办法令别人让着我，所以我不知道我用了多长时间才意识到我伤害了这么多人。我不仅得罪了很多要好的朋友，因为我总试图摆布他们；而且我还一次又一次地践踏了我生活中最珍贵的亲情：母女之情。

即使在我重获新生 10 年之后的今天，每当我回忆往事，我还是对从前的所作所为深感震惊：我总是用刻薄的话伤害和刺痛我所关爱的人，我总用迷茫的举动和愤怒的情绪左右我的行为——而我这么做只是为了顺着性子。

我的母亲是在 38 岁的时候不顾医生的警告生下我的，她总是哭着对我说，“我等了这么长时间才得到你，求你不要推开我，我想帮你。”

而我总会尖刻地回答说，“我没叫你这么做，我从没有想过要你关心我！让我一个人呆着，就当我死了吧！”

我母亲开始相信我是来真的，因为我的行为证明了这一点。

我很自私，总想支配别人，不惜一切手段只是为了我行我素。像许多高中女生那样，我首先约会的总是那些高不可攀的男生。我常常晚上很晚时瞒着母亲溜出去，仅仅想证明我能得手。我会毫不犹豫地编造出有眉有眼的谎话来，我会想方设法吸引别人的注意力，同时又设法摆出一副低姿态。

在我生命的那段时间里，我沉湎于毒品之中，吸毒改变了我的心灵和人格，正因为如此我脱口而出的话总是那么可怕、尖刻。然而，我迷恋的不是毒品。我所迷恋的仅仅是仇恨，我唯一的快感就是使别人痛苦。

然后，我开始问自己：为什么会这样，有什么必要伤害别人？为什么受伤的恰是我最关心的人？为什么要撒谎？为什么要伤害我的母亲？所有这些“为什么”让我发疯，直到有一天我再也受不了了，从一

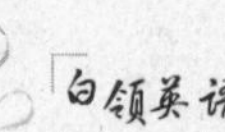

辆时速 80 英里的车上跳了下来。

第二天晚上，我躺在医院里无法入眠，我意识到我不想死。

我并不想给别人制造更多的痛苦来掩饰我想逃避的东西——那就是自我仇视，一种给别人带来痛苦的自我仇视。

多年来，我第一次看清了母亲痛苦的面孔，她温暖、疲惫的棕色眼睛中充满了对女儿新生的感激和对她等了 38 年才怀上的女儿的爱。

我第一次体验到无条件的母爱，这是一种多么强烈的感情啊！

尽管我对她撒了那么多的谎，她依然爱我。一天下午，我躺在她膝盖上哭了几个小时，我问她为什么我做了那么多的蠢事，她却依然爱着我？她低头望着我，拂去我脸上的头发，诚恳地说，“我不知道。”

慈祥的笑容透过眼泪从她的眼中流露出来，她那饱经岁月风霜的脸上的皱纹说明了一切。我是她的女儿，但更重要的是，她是我母亲。不是每一个堕落的孩子都像我这样幸运，不是每一个母亲都像我母亲那样一次次被逼上绝路却又一次次带着爱回到我身边。

无条件的爱是我们能够给予的最珍贵的礼物，过去的罪过得到原谅是我们能够得到的最宝贵的礼物。我敢说我们不可能在一生中两度体验这样纯洁的爱。

我以前多么地幸运呀！现在总算明白了。我想把从母亲那儿得到的礼物转送给世上所有迷茫、彷徨的失足青少年。

觉得痛苦、需要帮助、体验真爱，这些都是正常的，敞开心扉去迎接这一切吧。从坚硬的自我的外壳中解放出来，去呼吸生命的空气吧……

What Mother Taught Me

母亲的 教诲

Anonymous/佚名

My mother taught me to appreciate a job well done:

"If you're going to kill each other, do it outside. I just finished cleaning!"

My mother taught me religion:

"You'd better pray that will come out of the carpet."

My mother taught me about time travel:

"If you don't straighten up, I'm going to knock you into the middle of next week!"

My mother taught me logic:

"Because I said so, that's why!"

My mother taught me foresight:

"Be sure you wear clean underwear in case you're in an accident."

My mother taught me about contortion:

"Will you look at the dirt on the back of your neck!"

My mother taught me about stamina:

"You'll sit there 'til all that spinach is finished."

My mother taught me about weather:

"It looks as if a tornado swept through your room."

My mother taught me how to solve physics problems:

"If I yelled because I saw a meteor coming toward you, would you listen then?"

My mother taught me about hypocrisy:

"If I've told you once, I've told you a million times. Don't exaggerate!!!"

My mother taught me about envy:

"There are millions of less fortunate children in this world who don't have wonderful parents like you do!"

我母亲教我如何珍惜他人辛苦劳动：

"如果你们要打架，到外边打去——我刚整理好房间！"

我母亲教我什么是宗教：

"你最好祈祷那个东西能从地毯下冒出来。"

我母亲教我什么是时间旅行：

"你要是不改，我把你一把推到下周三！"（意为：不让过周末。）

我母亲教我什么是逻辑：

"为什么？因为我就是这么说的！"

我母亲教我什么是远见：

"一定要穿干净内衣，以防万一你遇到事故。"

我母亲教我什么是柔体杂技：

"你能不能看看你脖子后面的泥！"

我母亲教我什么是耐力：

"坐在那儿，直到把所有的菠菜吃完。"

我母亲教我认识天气：

"好像有龙卷风席卷过你的房间。"

我母亲教我如何解决物理学问题：

"如果我高声叫喊，是因为我看见有一颗流星正朝你俯冲而来，那你会不会听我的话？"

我母亲教我什么是伪善：

"如果我曾告诉过你一次，我实际上已告诉过你一百万次——不许夸张！！！"

我母亲教我什么是嫉妒：

"这世界上有数百万不幸的孩子，他们可没有你这么好的父母！"

What Motherhood Really Means

母性的真谛

Anonymous/佚名

Time is running out for my friend. While we are sitting at lunch she casually mentions she and her husband are thinking of starting a family. "We're taking a survey," she says, half-joking. "Do you think I should have a baby?"

"It will change your life," I say, carefully keeping my tone neutral. "I know," she says, "no more sleeping in on weekends, no more spontaneous holidays..."

But that's not what I mean at all. I look at my friend, trying to decide what to tell her. I want her to know what she will never learn in childbirth classes. I want to tell her that the physical wounds of child bearing will heal, but becoming a mother will leave her with an emotional wound so raw that she will be vulnerable forever.

I consider warning her that she will never again read a newspaper without thinking: "What if that had been MY child?" That every plane crash, every house fire will haunt her. That when she sees pictures of starving children, she will wonder if anything could be worse than watching your child die. I look at her carefully manicured nails and stylish suit and think that no matter how sophisticated she is, becoming a mother will reduce her to the primitive level of a bear protecting her cub.

I feel I should warn her that no matter how many years she has invested in

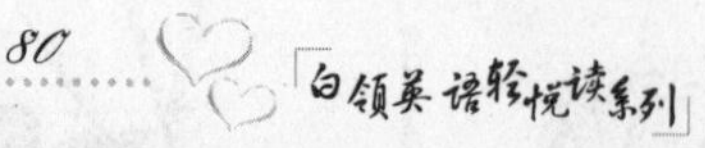

her career, she will be professionally derailed by motherhood. She might arrange for child care, but one day she will be going into an important business meeting, and she will think her baby's sweet smell. She will have to use every ounce of discipline to keep from running home, just to make sure her child is all right.

I want my friend to know that every decision will no longer be routine. That a five-year-old boy's desire to go to the men's room rather than the women's at a restaurant will become a major dilemma. The issues of independence and gender identity will be weighed against the prospect that a child molester may be lurking in the lavatory. However decisive she may be at the office, she will second-guess herself constantly as a mother.

Looking at my attractive friend, I want to assure her that eventually she will shed the added weight of pregnancy, but she will never feel the same about herself. That her own life, now so important, will be of less value to her once she has a child. She would give it up in a moment to save her offspring, but will also begin to hope for more years — not to accomplish her own dreams — but to watch her children accomplish theirs.

I want to describe to my friend the exhilaration of seeing your child learn to hit a ball. I want to capture for her the belly laugh of a baby who is touching the soft fur of a dog for the first time. I want her to taste the joy that is so real it hurts.

My friend's look makes me realize that tears have formed in my eyes. "You'll never regret it," I say finally. Then, squeezing my friend's hand, I offer a prayer for her and me and all of the mere mortal women who stumble their way into this holiest of callings.

时光荏苒，朋友已经老大不小了。我们坐在一起吃饭的时候，她漫不经心地提到她和她的丈夫正考虑要小孩。“我们正在做一项调查，”她半开玩笑地说，“你觉得我应该要个小孩吗？”

“他将改变你的生活。”我小心翼翼地说道，尽量使语气保持客观。“这我知道。”她答道，“周末睡不成懒觉，再也不能随心所欲休假了……”

但我说的绝非这些。我注视着朋友，试图整理一下自己的思绪。我想让她知道她永远不可能在分娩课上学到的东西。我想让她知道：分娩的有形伤疤可以愈合，但是做母亲的情感伤痕却永远如新，她会因此变得十分脆弱。

我想告诫她：做了母亲后，每当她看报纸时就会情不自禁地联想："如果那件事情发生在我的孩子身上将会怎样啊！"每一次飞机失事、每一场住宅火灾都会让她提心吊胆。看到那些忍饥挨饿的孩子们的照片时，她会思索：世界上还有什么比眼睁睁地看着自己的孩子饿死更惨的事情呢？我打量着她精修细剪的指甲和时尚前卫的衣服，心里想到：不管她打扮多么考究，做了母亲后，她会变得像护崽的母熊那样原始而不修边幅。

我觉得自己应该提醒她，不管她在事业上投入了多少年，一旦做了母亲，工作就会脱离常规。她自然可以安排他人照顾孩子，但说不定哪天她要去参加一个非常重要的商务会议，却忍不住想起宝宝身上散发的甜甜乳香。她不得不拼命克制自己，才不至于为了看看孩子是否安然无恙而中途回家。

我想告诉朋友，有了孩子后，她将再也不能按照惯例作出决定。在餐馆，5岁的儿子想进男厕而不愿进女厕将成为摆在她眼前的一大难题：她将在两个选择之间权衡一番：尊重孩子的独立和性别意识，还是让他进男厕所冒着被潜在的儿童性骚扰者侵害的危险？任凭她在办公室多么果断，作为母亲，她仍经常后悔自己当时的决定。

注视着我的这位漂亮的朋友，我想让她明确地知道，她最终会恢复到怀孕前的体重，但是她对自己的感觉已然不同。她现在视为如此重要的生命将随着孩子的诞生而变得不那么宝贵。为了救自己的孩子，她时刻愿意献出自己的生命。但她也开始希望多活一些年头，不是为了实现自己的梦想，而是为了看着孩子们美梦成真。

我想向朋友形容自己看到孩子学会击球时的喜悦之情。我想让她留意宝宝第一次触摸狗的绒毛时的捧腹大笑。我想让她品尝快乐，尽管这快乐真实得令人心痛。

朋友的表情让我意识到自己已经是热泪盈眶。"你永远不会后悔，"我最后说。然后紧紧地握住朋友的手，为她、为自己、也为每一位艰难跋涉、准备响应母亲职业神圣的召唤的平凡女性献上自己的祈祷。

All You Remember
走过人生你所记得的事

Anonymous/佚名

All you remember about your child being two is never using the restroom alone or getting to watch a movie without talking animals. You recall afternoons talking on the phone while crouching in the bedroom closet, and being convinced your child would be the first ivy League college student to graduate wearing pullovers at the ceremony. You remember worrying about the bag of M&M's melting in your pocket and ruining your good dress. You wished for your child to be more independent.

孩子2岁时，你所记得的，是从不能独自使用卫生间，从不看一部与动物无关的电影。你记得那些蜷缩在卧室储衣间跟朋友通电话的下午，深信你的孩子将是第一个身着套头衫出席毕业典礼的常春藤名牌大学的毕业生。你记得你担心那袋M&M巧克力糖会在你的衣兜里融化，毁了你体面的衣服。你多希望你的孩子更独立些。

All you remember about your child being five is the first day of school and finally having the house to yourself. You remember joining the PTA and being elected president when you left a meeting to use the restroom. You remember being asked "Is Santa real?" and saying "Yes" because he had to be for a little bit longer. You remember shaking the sofa cushions for loose change, so the toothfairy could come and take away your child's first lost tooth. You wished for your child to have all permanent teeth.

孩子5岁时，你所记得的，是他上学第一天你终于独自拥有整个房子了。你记得参加家长——教师联系会，在你离开会议室去洗手间时，你当选为会长。你记得孩子问你“圣诞老人是真的吗?”你回答“是的”，因为他还需要你的肯定回答，尽管不久他就能自己判断了。你记得在沙发垫子下一通翻腾要找出些零钱，这样牙齿仙女就会把你孩子掉的第一颗牙带走。你多希望孩子的牙都换成了恒牙。

All you remember about your child being seven is the carpool schedule. You learned to apply makeup in two minutes and brush your teeth in the rearview mirror because the only time you had to yourself was when you were stopped at red lights. You considered painting your car yellow and posting a "taxi" sign on the lawn next to the garage door. You remember people staring at you, the few times you were out of the car, because you kept flexing your foot and making acceleration noises. You wished for the day your child would learn how to drive.

孩子7岁时，你所记得的，是合伙用车的时间安排。你学会了在两分钟内化完妆，照着汽车后视镜刷牙，因为你能给自己找出的时间就只有汽车停在红灯前的那小段。你想过把你的车子漆成黄色，并在车库门旁的草坪上立一个“出租车”的标志牌。你记得有几次你下车后，人们盯着你，因为你不断用脚踩油门加速，制造噪音。你多希望孩子有一天能学会开车。

All you remember about your child being ten is managing the school fund raisers. You sold wrapping paper for paint, T-shirts for new furniture, and magazine subscriptions for shade trees in the school playground.

孩子10岁时，你所记得的，是怎样组织学校的募捐者。你们为重新粉刷学校兜售包装纸，为购置新家具兜售T恤衫，为在学校操场上种植遮阳树劝人订阅各种杂志。

You remember storing a hundred cases of candy bars in the garage to sell so the school band could get new uniforms, and how they melted together on an unseasonably warm spring afternoon. You wished your child would grow out of playing an instrument.

你记得你在车库里存放了上百盒糖果等待出售，得到钱后学校的乐队就可以购置新制服，可是那些糖果竟在一个暖和得过头的春天的下午全都融化在一起了。你多希望孩子长大，不再演奏什么乐器了。

All you remember about your child being twelve is sitting in the stands during baseball practice and hoping your child's team would strike out fast because you had more important things to do at home. The coach didn't understand how busy you were. You wished the baseball season would be over soon.

孩子12岁时，你所记得的，是孩子在体育场打棒球练习赛时，你坐在看台上希望孩子所在的队很快三击不中出局，因为家里还有更重要的事等你去做。教练不明白你为什么那么忙。你多希望棒球赛季能尽快结束。

All you remember about your child being fourteen is being asked not to stop the car in front of the school in the morning. You had to drive two blocks further and unlock the doors without coming to a complete stop. You remember not getting to kiss your child goodbye or talking to him in front of his friends. You wished your child would be more mature.

孩子14岁时，你所记得的，是他不让你早晨把汽车停在校门口。你不得不开过两个街区，车还没停稳就赶紧打开车门。你记得不能在他的朋友面前跟他吻别或说话。你多希望孩子能更成熟些。

All you remember about your child being sixteen is loud music and undecipherable lyrics screamed to a rhythmic beat. You wished for your child to grow up and leave home with the stereo.

孩子16岁时，你所记得的，是吵闹的音乐和以富有节奏的拍子尖声唱出的难以听懂的歌词。你多希望孩子快点长大成人，带着音响离开家。

All you remember about your child being eighteen is the day they were born and having all the time in the world.

孩子18岁时，你所记得的，是他们出生的那一天，拥有世界所有的时光。

And, as you walk through your quiet house, you wonder where they went and you wish your child hadn't grown up so fast.

当你在静静的房子里走来走去时，你纳闷他们去哪里了——你多希望孩子别这么快就长大了。

Better Late than Never

迟做总比不做好

Anonymous/佚名

Papa's jaw dropped when mama told him that Sister had cheated on her final exams — not to succeed but to fail. "It's unbelievable!" he said. "Sister has always been so proud of her good grades!"

"Yes, she has," said Mama. "But it's not unbelievable. It just shows how badly she wanted off the swimming team."

"Wanted off the swimming team?" said Papa. "She never said anything about that to me."

"Of course she didn't," said Mama. "She was afraid you'd blow your top. You already had her getting a swimming scholarship to college and winning gold medals at the Olympics. Can you imagine how much pressure she must have felt? For her, being on the team couldn't have been much fun."

"Oh, my gosh!" Papa said, clapping a hand to his forehead. "I've been so stupid! I just thought she'd want to be a champion swimmer because she's so good at it."

"It's like anything else, dear," said Mama. "No matter how good at it you are, if it stops being fun, you won't want to do it anymore."

Papa put his head in his hands.

"She must be really mad at me," he mumbled. "Maybe I should say sorry to her."

妈妈告诉爸爸姐姐在期末考试中作弊被抓不及格时爸爸的下颌都要掉下来了。“这不可能”，他说道，“她的成绩一向很好啊！”

“是的，没错”，妈妈说，“但这也不那么难以置信。这只表明了她有多么想退出游泳队。”

“退出游泳队？”爸爸说，“她从来没有跟我说过这件事啊。”

“她当然没有。”妈妈说，“她害怕你会发脾气。你已经让她拿到了一份大学里的游泳奖学金，还在奥运会拿到了金牌。您能想象得到她承受了多大的压力吗？对她来说，再待在游泳队里已没有多少乐趣可言了。”

“噢，上帝。”爸爸说道，手掌一拍前额，“我怎么就这么蠢呢？我只是觉得她游泳很出色，肯定想成为一名冠军选手。”

“这是另外一回事，亲爱的。”妈妈说，“不管你有多么出色，如果你不再感兴趣，你便不会再继续做下去了。”

爸爸埋下了头去。

“她一定在怪我。”他咕哝着，“也许我该向她道歉。”

Sister's footsteps could be heard on the stairs. She came into the kitchen and looked hopefully up at her parents.

"Honey," said Mama with a smile, "Your papa and I have decided that there's no reason for you to be on the swimming team if you don't want to."

Sister's face lit up like a Christmas tree. "Yippee!" she cried.

"And," added Papa, "there's no need for any more drills. I'm sure you'll bring your grades back up all by yourself."

Sister ran to Papa and jumped into his arms. She gave him a big hug. "I'm going to go play cards with Lizzy!" she said. "See you later!"

From the kitchen window, Mama and papa watched their daughter run down the sunny road toward Lizzy's house.

"It's good to see her happy again," said Mama.

"It sure is," Papa agreed. "As for the swimming team, there's always next year."

"If?" Mama prompted him.

"Oh, right," said Papa. If she wants to.

Mama smiled. "At least you're learning, dear," she said. She kissed him.

"Well, you know what they say," Papa said. "Better late than never."

楼梯那里传来了姐姐的脚步声。她走进厨房，充满希望地看着她的父母。

“亲爱的，”妈妈微笑着，“我和你爸爸觉得如果你不愿意的话，你没有理由再呆在游泳队里了。”

姐姐的脸如同圣诞树一般被点亮了。“耶!”她叫到。

“还有，”爸爸说到，“你也没必要继续训练了。我相信你自己能够把成绩提上去的。”

姐姐朝爸爸跑去，一把抱住了他。“我要和 Lizzy 打牌去了!”她说，“回见。”

穿过厨房的窗户，妈妈和爸爸看着他们的女儿在洒满阳光的大路上朝着 Lizzy 的家跑去。

“看到她重新高兴起来真好。”妈妈说。

“那当然，”爸爸赞同道，“游泳队的话，明年也还是可以的。”

“如果?”妈妈提示他。

“哦，对了。”如果她愿意的话。

妈妈笑道，“至少你在进步了，亲爱的。”她说道。她吻了他。

“好了，你知道他们说什么了。”爸爸说，“迟做总比不做好。”

The Tollefson Boy Goes to College

托勒家小子上大学

Anonymous/佚名

In a little while, the Tollefson boy's going to get into the chevy with his mother. And they're going to pick up his aunt Mary and grandma and his great uncle Senator Kay Torvellts. And all of them are going to drive into St. Cloud where he is to register for the fall term at St. Cloud State University.

"Why? Why? It's just registration," he's told his mother. "It's like getting a driver's license. It takes about ten minutes. Why do we have to take everybody with us?"

She says, "Because they're proud of you. They want to be there."

"Oh," he says. "Why don't you just take them and leave me at home?"

"Oh no, Johnny," she says. "You're the one who's getting registered for college."

He thinks about the Flambeauxs as they drive into St. Cloud, him in the front seat squeezed in between grandma and his mother driving, his Uncle Senator Torvolts in the back seat with Aunt Mary. All the windows are rolled up, because grandma can't stand drafts. And they're all talking at the same time and saying dumb things.

Aunt Mary reads billboards out loud. You already know what they're saying but she reads them even down the highway. And there in front of them is a house being carried on a flatbed truck down the highway, and they get up behind it and Aunt Mary says, "Well, look at that, Johnny! There's a house on the highway.

Isn't that a deal!"

"Look at them, horses over there, Johnny! My! What a whole bunch of them!"

"Ah, it's a warm day today, isn't it, Johnny?"

And his great uncle in the back seat! Whoever had a great uncle whose first name was Senator? How to explain to people that his mother just named him Senator because she felt it was a good name?

And he's sitting in the back seat and he's talking a mile a minute even though everybody else is talking. He's saying, "Oh, what a wonderful day it is today, Johnny! Ahh, boy, you're going to remember this day the rest of your life. Oh, the sun is shinning! Oh, God is good, Johnny."

Finally they come up towards the campus and he's crouching lower and lower in the front seat, ducking his head and putting his hand up to his face. What if somebody sees him with this bunch?

Around and round they go, looking for a parking space. Up one street down the other around the block three, four times and finally his mother says, "Oh gracious! I don't know what to do. Should I park downtown and walk or should I double park or..."

Johnny said, "No!" He said, "Just stop here." He said, "I'll run in and it will only take me a couple of minutes. You all stay in the car."

And he jumps out of the car right over his grandma and runs as fast as he can go up the walk and into the building. Poor child. He really wants them to run after and catch up with him, but they won't today. Some day they will.

Meanwhile they sit there in the car, Aunt Mary and Senator K. in the back seat and Momma and grandma in the front. And Senator is saying, "Ah, it's a wonderful day! He's a good boy. He's going to do well. I'm proud I was here to see it!"

再过一会儿，托勒家小子和他妈妈就有的忙了。他们要去接玛丽姨妈和姥姥还有舅姥爷参议员·凯·托威茨。然后他们全体开车到圣克劳去，因为托勒家小子要到圣克劳大学报到秋季入学。

“为什么？为什么？不过是注个册嘛，”他对妈妈说，“那跟拿驾驶执照一样。只用10分钟时间。为什么必须人人到场？”

她说：“因为他们为你感到骄傲啊。他们都想到场。”

“哦，”他说，“不如你带他们去，把我留在家里好了。”

“噢，这可不行，尊尼，”她说，“要去学校报到的人是你。”

他们驱车前往圣克劳，他挤在车前位，在姥姥和他妈妈的中间，心里想着弗雷标克思一家。舅老爷参议员·托威茨和玛丽姨妈坐在后座上，所有的窗子都摇了上去，因为姥姥受不了车风。而且他们同时发言，说着无聊的话。

玛丽姨妈大声地念着广告牌上的字。你已经知道广告牌上说什么了，可她还是要念出来，甚至是一路念。公路前方有辆卡车拖着一座屋子走下高速公路，他们在后面立起身来看，玛丽姨妈说：“啊，看啊，尊尼！路上有个房子。可不是件大事吗！”

“看啊，尊尼，那边有马！天哪，一大群马啊！”

“啊，天气多暖和啊，是不是，尊尼？”

还有这位坐在后座的舅姥爷！谁的舅姥爷会起名叫参议员呢？怎样去跟别人解释，他妈妈给他起名叫参议员是因为她觉得这名字好听？

他正坐在后座上滔滔不绝，尽管其他人也都在说着话。他说：“噢，今天天气多好啊，尊尼！噢，老天，你一辈子都会记住这一天的。噢，阳光灿烂！噢，太好了，尊尼。”

他们终于进了校园，他在前座越坐越低，埋着头，捂着脸。万一给人看到他和这一家子人在一起怎么办？

他们转了一圈又一圈找停车位。绕着街区开过一条又一条街道，兜了三四圈后，他妈妈说道：“哦，老天！我没办法了。是停到市区然后走路呢，还是靠别人的车停，还是……”

尊尼说：“不！”他说：“停这好了。”他说：“我跑过去只要几分钟。你们全待在车里。”

然后他越过姥姥跳下车去，飞快地跑起来，跑上人行道，跑进大楼里——可怜的孩子。他多么希望他们跟上来赶上他，可他们今天却没有。以后他们会的。

与此同时，他们正坐在车里，玛丽姨妈和舅姥爷参议员·凯坐在后座，妈妈和姥姥坐在前座。参议员说道：“啊，天气真好！他是个好孩子。他能办好事情。能亲眼见证，我感到太骄傲了！”

He little knew the sorrow that was in his vacant chair,
He never guessed they'd miss him, or he'd surely have been there;
He couldn't see his mother or the lump that filled her throat,
Or the tears that started falling as she read his hasty note;
And he couldn't see his father, sitting sorrowful and dumb,
Or he never would have written that he thought he couldn't come.

He little knew the gladness that his presence would have made,
And the joy it would have given, or he never would have stayed.
He didn't know how hungry had the little mother grown
Once again to see her baby and to claim him for her own.
He didn't guess the meaning of his visit Christmas Day
Or he never would have written that he couldn't get away.

He couldn't see the fading of the cheeks that once were pink,
And the silver in the tresses; and he didn't stop to think
How the years are passing swiftly, and next Christmas it might be
There would be no home to visit and no mother dear to see.
He didn't think about it I'll not say he didn't care.
He was heedless and forgetful or he'd surely have been there.

他那空闲椅子上的悲伤，他知之甚少，
从未想过自己会被想念，也未想过应该回去；
他看不见他的母亲，也看不到那在喉的哽咽，
更看不到，母亲读他草就的便条时老泪纵横；
他看不到他的父亲，一人孤坐，百无聊赖，
否则他也就不应该写下，他可能回不去了。

他的出现会带去的欢乐，他知之甚少，
他理应给予的欢乐，却从未停留。
他不知道母亲已经变得多么渴望，
渴望再次看到她的孩子，给他久违的母爱。
他未曾想过圣诞回家的意义，
否则他也就不应该写下，他可能回不去了。

他看不见曾经的红润的双颊如今是何等消瘦，
看不到黑发中的一缕银丝；他未曾停下来想一想，
时光如何飞逝，到了下个圣诞节，
可能再没有家可回，再没有亲爱的母亲可见。
他未曾想过——我不会说他不关心这些。
他只是粗心而且健忘，否则他肯定会在家里。

Are you going home for Christmas? Have you written you'll be there?
Going home to kiss the mother and to show her that you care?
Going home to greet the father in a way to make him glad?
If you're not I hope there'll never come a time you'll wish you had.
Just sit down and write a letter it will make their heart strings hum
With a tune of perfect gladness if you'll tell them that you'll come.

你圣诞节回家吗？写了信告诉父母你会回去吗？
回家亲吻你的妈妈，向她表示关心？
回家问候爸爸，使他高兴？
如果你还没有，我希望为时未晚。
坐下来，写封信——你的心弦会响起
完美快乐的音符——如果你告诉他们，你会回家。

Family Motto

朱子家训品读

Anonymous/佚名

一粥一饭，当思来之不易；

半丝半缕，恒念物力维艰。

The growing of rice and of grain
Think on whenever you dine;
Remember how silk is obtained
Which keeps you warm and looks fine.

宜未雨而绸缪，勿临渴而掘井。

In periods of drought
Wise birds mend their nest
So when the clouds burst
They snugly may rest;
Never be the fool
Who starts to dig a well in the ground
When he wants a drink of water
And water can't be found.

与肩挑贸易毋占便宜，
与贫苦亲邻须加温恤。
Bargain you not with the traveler who vends;
Share of your wealth with your neighbors and friends.

居家戒争讼，讼则终凶；
处世戒多言，言多必失。
Don't take into court your family disputes,
Unpleasant endings emerge from lawsuits;
To comport yourself well in society,
Restrain loose tongue's impropriety.

勿恃权势而凌孤寡；
勿贪口腹而恣杀性。
Use not your bow and arrow
To bully orphan and widow.
Do not dumb animals slaughter at will
Your appetite greedy to over fulfill.

乖僻自是，悔悟必多；
颓惰自甘，家园终替。
Egocentric people grow
Much regret and sorrow;
Lazy, slothful people sow
Poverty tomorrow.

施惠勿念；受恩莫忘。

In proclaiming your virtues go slow;

And be mindful of mercy you own.

凡事当留余地，

得意不宜再往。

Leave room for retreat

When trying new feat.

You will try, try in vain

To repeat windfall gain.

人有喜庆，不可生忌妒心；

人有祸患，不可生欣幸心。

Don't envy other's success;

Don't gloat o'er other's distress.

善欲人见，不是真善；

恶恐人知，便是大恶。

To brag of the good you have done

Will never impress anyone.

Personal scandals you try hard to hide

Will soon be known far and wide.

My Safe Child
我那安全的孩子

Daphna Baram/达夫纳·巴拉姆

I am thirty-three years old, and I am so happy that I am not a mother. I do not hear a biological clock ticking, only the nerve wrecking ticks of bombs yet to explode. My friends are leaping whenever their cell phones ring. "Where are you? No, you can't go out. No, I don't care if all the other children are going." How naive children are when they tell lies. What mother in Israel now would believe that "all the children are going" anywhere?

And where are the children going? Where will their fears take them? In many places in the world children are afraid of the unknown, of the unreal. You know that you live in a war zone when you realize that the greatest fears of the children are of what they know only too well.

Two years ago, when my younger brother was ten, he came home from school, and as he opened the door he heard the familiar sound of explosion rising from the street he just left behind him. Sitting in front of the television five minutes later, he could see his friend wandering blindly in the street, which was covered with body parts and injured people. The friend's father, who picked him up from school and took him for a pizza, was killed in front of his eyes. My brother refused to talk about it. "This kid wasn't really a friend of mine," is all he would say, "I don't really know him that well." That evening he told my father that he is afraid of Freddy Kruger, a monstrous murderer from a common horror film. My father didn't know whether to laugh or cry, but I suspect he felt some relief. How good it is to caress your child's hair and to tell him that Kruger doesn't really exist.

But the man who exploded himself in the centre of a busy street did exist. And the man who will explode himself in another one of our busy streets in a few years is now my brother's age. His mother doesn't have to worry about the dangers which lurk on the way to school. There are no schools anymore. We have demolished them all, when we crushed the infrastructure of the Palestinian Authority. His younger brother was killed when our soldiers exploded their home. Our soldiers exploded their home because his older brother was a "wanted person". Exploding his family's home was our way to insure that he will soon turn from a wanted person into an unwanted body, torn to a thousand pieces, surrounded by his victims.

The young terrorist to be sleeps now in a tent provided by UNRWA. What is he afraid of? Not much to fear anymore. The worst already took place. But the bulldozers are still around, demolishing the neighbours' homes. Every day a few new tents join the raw. His mother tells him how they were deported from their home in Latrun in 1967. His grandmother tells him it was nothing compared to what she had to go through when she was driven away from Jaffa in 1948, carrying his screaming mother, then a newborn, in her arms.

My grandmother doesn't understand her plight. It had never occurred to her to go back to her home in Poland, which she had to flee as a refugee, haunted by the rise of Nazism in Europe. The fact that the Palestinians still talk about Jaffa, she says, just proves that they want to exterminate us. Whenever a suicide

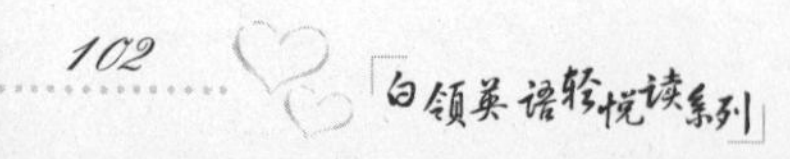

bombing strikes our cities, my grandmother calls me and tells me of her secret plan. "I am an old woman, and I have nothing to loose," she says in a conspiratorial tone. "I will wear rags like their women, and go and explode myself in the centre of Nablus. This will teach them a lesson. I will show them what it's like." I am trying to tell her that they already know what it is like, that the number of their dead is three times bigger than ours, that the fear and terror we spread in their lives is much bigger than ours. But my grandmother doesn't hear me, because she is crying. "They are not human beings," she says. "What people can do such things, kill children like this?" De-humanised people, I want to answer, but I keep my mouth shut, and think about the child that I don't want to have.

The child I won't have will never feel the guilt of being an occupier, or the fear of becoming a victim. I will never tell him not to be scared, when fear is the only rational thing to feel. I will not have to teach him that the Palestinian child is a human being just like him, while everybody else will tell him that it is not so. The child I won't have will keep sleeping, curled in a secret corner of my mind. The child I will never have is going to be the only safe child in the Middle East.

我今年33岁，很高兴没有成为一名母亲。我听不见生物钟的滴答作响，只听到即将爆炸的炸弹那令人神经崩溃的走秒声。我的朋友们一听到自己的手机铃响就会惊跳起来。“你在哪里？不行，你不能出去。不行，我才不管是不是别的孩子都去呢。”孩子们撒谎时是多么地天真啊。如今在以色列会有什么母亲相信“所有孩子都去”哪个地方呢？

那么，孩子们要去哪儿呢？他们的恐惧会将他们带往哪儿呢？在世界上许多地方，孩子们害怕的是那些未知的、不真实的东西。而当你意识到孩子们最恐惧的恰恰是那些他们最为熟知的事物时，你知道你是生活在战区。

两年前我的弟弟10岁，他放学回家，刚打开门，就听见熟悉的爆炸声从他身后刚刚离开的街上响起。5分钟后坐在电视机前，他看到了他的朋友在满是伤者和残肢断臂的街上茫然地徘徊。朋友的父亲刚把他从学校接出来还带他去吃了比萨饼，现在就眼睁睁地被杀死了。我弟弟拒绝谈论这件事。“这个小孩并不真是我的朋友，”他老那么说，“我跟他真的不是很熟。”那天晚上，他跟我父亲说他害怕弗莱迪·克鲁格，这个人物是一部大家都熟悉的恐怖片里的杀人恶魔。我父亲不知道是该笑还是该哭，但我猜想他感到了某种宽慰。抚摸着孩子的头发告诉他克鲁格并非真地存在，这种感觉有多棒。

然而，那个在繁忙的街道中央将自身引爆的人确实存在。而那个几年后将要在我们另一条繁忙街道上引爆自己的人现在正是我弟弟的年纪。他的母亲无需担心潜伏在上学路上的危险，因为根本就不再有学校，在我们破坏巴勒斯坦基础设施时已经将学校全部摧毁了。他的弟弟在我们的战士炸毁他们家时死去了。我们的战士炸毁他们家是因为他的哥哥是个被通缉的要犯。我们用炸毁他家屋子这个办法来确保他那位哥哥能很快从一个被通缉的要犯变为没人要的尸体，被炸成了千百片，旁边都是因他而受害的人。

这个未来的小恐怖分子现在就睡在联合国难民救济及工程局提供的帐篷里。他害怕什么呢？再也没多少令他害怕的了，最糟糕的事情已经发生。然而，推土机仍然在周围拆除邻居家的屋子。每天都有几顶新的帐篷加入到这种未开化的生活中来。他的母亲告诉他，1967年他们是如何被驱逐出在拉特伦的家的。他的姥姥告诉他，1948 年她被从雅法赶出来，怀抱着那当时刚出生不久哇哇直哭的他的母亲，现在的情况比起那时经历的一切算不了什么。

我的祖母不了解自己所处的境况。她在纳粹主义肆虐欧洲时以难民的身份逃离了波兰，之后她从未想过要重返那里的家。她说，巴勒斯坦人仍在谈论雅法只是说明了他们想消灭我们。每当我们城市发生一起自杀性爆炸，我祖母就会打电话跟我讲她的秘密计划。“我是个老太婆，没有什么放不下的。”她以阴谋策划的语气说道，“我穿上像他们女人那样的破衣服，到纳布卢斯市中心去引爆自己，给他们个教训，让他们看看这像什么样子。”我试图告诉她，他们已经知道这像什么样子，告诉她，他们的死亡人数比我们多3倍，告诉她，我们在他们生活中播撒的害怕和恐怖要比我们自己生活中的多得多。但祖母听不见我的话，因为她在哭。“他们不是人，”她说，“什么人会做这样的事，像这样杀孩子?”没有人性的人，我想回答，但我没有张嘴，心里想着我那不想生养的孩子。

我不想生养的这个孩子将永远不会为自己成为占领者而感到有罪，也不会为自己可能成为受害者而感到害怕。我将永远不用告诉他不要怕，尽管害怕是现在唯一合乎理性的感受。我将不必教导他巴勒斯坦孩子也是像他一样的人，而其他所有人都会告诉他并非如此。这个我不想生养的孩子将蜷缩在我的大脑内一个秘密角落里一直睡大觉。这个我不想生养的孩子将是中东地区唯一安全的孩子。

The Easter Bunny

复活节兔子

Beth H. Arbogast

贝丝.H. 艾伯嘉斯特

When I was a little girl, every Sunday my family of six would put on their best clothes and go to Sunday School and then church. The kids in elementary school would all meet together to sing songs, and then later divide into groups based on their ages.

One Easter Sunday, all the kids arrived with big eyes and big stories about what the Easter Bunny had brought. While all of the kids shared their stories with delight, one young boy, whom I will call Bobby, sat sullenly. One of the teachers, noticing this, said to him, "And what did the Easter Bunny bring you?" He replied, "My mom locked the door on accident so the Easter Bunny couldn't get inside."

This sounded like a reasonable idea to all of us kids, so we kept on going with the stories. My mom knew the true story, though. Bobby's mom was a single parent, and she suspected that they just couldn't afford the Easter Bunny.

After Sunday School was over, everyone went off to church. When my dad came to meet us my mom announced that we were going home instead. At home, she explained that to make Bobby feel better, we were going to pretend to be the Easter Bunny and make a basket of goodies for him and leave it at church. We all donated some of our candies to the basket, and headed back up to church. There, mom unzipped his coat, hung the basket over the hanger, and zipped up the coat and attached a note.

Dear Bobby,

I'm sorry I missed your house last night. Happy Easter.

Love,

The Easter Bunny.

当我还是个小女孩儿的时候，每个星期天我们一家六口就会换上各自最好的衣服去参加主日学校，然后去教堂。小学的孩子会在一起唱歌，然后根据年龄分组。

复活节的时候，所有的孩子来的时候都带着大眼睛和有关复活节兔子带来什么的故事。当所有的孩子都带着喜悦分享他们的故事时，一个小男孩，我们叫他鲍比，阴沉地坐在那儿。有位老师注意到了他，跟他说："复活节兔子给你带来什么了啊？"他回答道："我妈妈不小心锁上了门，复活节兔子进不来了。"

对于所有孩子来说，这是个说得过去的理由，于是我们继续我们的故事。但是我妈妈知道真正的故事。鲍比的妈妈是个单身母亲，她怀疑他们可能负担不起复活节兔子。

主日学校结束之后，每个人都去了教堂。当爸爸过来接我们时，妈妈说我们不去教堂而是回家。在家里她解释说为了让鲍比快乐一些，我们要假装是复活节兔子，然后装一篮子糖果放在教堂。我们都把自己的糖果拿了一些出来，然后回到了教堂。在那儿妈妈拉开衣服的拉链，把篮子挂在衣架上，再拉上拉链并留了一张字条：

亲爱的鲍比，

很抱歉昨天晚上错过了你的房子。复活节快乐。

爱你的，

复活节兔子。

Without a Nightlight

无灯之夜

Anonymous/佚名

The moon shone down on the lake like a spotlight. It was a warm summer evening, and I found the night sky, with its lightening stars, relaxing to watch. Five of us were sitting on the dock, wishing we could go for a swim. Paul asked Chelsea and me if we wanted to get on a big yellow tube and go across the cove. It sounded like fun.

We were on the tube, paddling across the lake, when Chelsea said that she was having doubts. Was it safe crossing the lake in this tube? Paul said he had done this before and that there was nothing to worry about. The boat speed limit was five miles an hour and all boats needed to have at least two lights on.

We were cruising along when, suddenly, Kari started yelling from the dock, saying she heard a boat coming. We didn't think anything about it, figuring we were on the opposite side from where the boat would be. Then suddenly, the noise became loud enough for us to hear over our splashing feet. We all began to panic.

We yelled back to the dock, asking them if they could see a boat, but no one could. So we kept going until the roar was louder than our voices. Then, all of a sudden, Kari started screaming, "Come back!" Her voice sounded scared, so we desperately started looking for a boat. Out of nowhere, over the roar of the

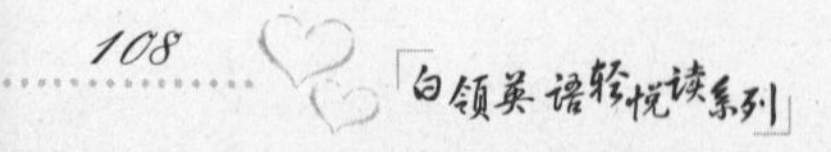

engine and the kicking of our feet, Kari yelled, "Oh my God, there's a boat!" The way she said it terrified me and I started to cry. None of us knew what to do.

We stayed as still as we could. Chelsea and I were on the tube. She was on my left and Paul was on my right, floating in the water. Once we were still, all I could hear was my heart pounding, the yelling all around me, and the roar of a boat coming closer and closer every second. Then suddenly, right in front of me, was my worst nightmare. There, just a few feet away, was the boat. It was coming right at us!

Chelsea froze right in her spot, screaming. I pushed her into the water and jumped in after her, just in time to save my own life. As I went under the water, I felt the boat skidding over my shoulder like a jet.

I looked up through the water, but at first I could not find the surface. Finally, I got to the top and took the biggest breath I've ever taken. But the terrifying situation was not over. The boat came back, looking for what it had struck, and almost hit us again.

Chelsea was above the water by the time I came up, and I could hear her yelling for Paul and me. I answered her, but Paul did not. It seemed as though we were calling for Paul forever, but thinking back, it was only about twenty seconds. At last, Paul came to the surface, and we made it back to the dock. Kari had to pull me in with the life rope because I felt like I could not move. Once we all got onto the dock, one of the men who was in the boat brought our tube in for us.

Paul kept saying that it was all his fault and that he was to blame for us almost being killed. We assured him that we had made the decision to go and he was not to blame. We sat on the dock telling our own versions of what had happened. The only way that our stories differed was the way the boat hit all of us. The boat hit me on the shoulder while I was trying to push off the bottom of the boat. Chelsea pushed off the boat with her hands; Paul got hit on the head.

Everyone agreed that I had saved Chelsea by pushing her off the tube.

The next afternoon, which was Father's Day, my parents and I went over to Paul's house to have a cookout. When we were all sitting on the dock, we told them our story. I spent a lot of that day thinking about how lucky we were just to be alive. That moment gave me nightmares for almost a year. To this day, I can still see the color of the waves and feel the way my heart was beating when I finally came up for air. That was one experience that I will never forget.

Without a doubt, the next time we go out on the lake at night, we'll bring along a light!

月亮如聚光灯般直射着湖面。那是个暖和的夏夜，我看到群星闪烁的夜空正悠悠闲闲地瞧着我们5个人。我们坐在码头上，一心盼着去游泳。保罗问切尔西和我想不想坐在一只大黄气胎上划过小湖湾。这听起来是个挺有趣的主意。

我们坐到气胎上，荡桨划过湖面，切尔西边说出她的顾虑：坐气胎过湖安不安全？保罗说他以前就这么做过，没什么好怕的。当时的船速都被控制在每小时5英里（约合8公里）内，所有的船上都应该至少配备两盏灯。

我们向前行驶着，突然间，卡丽在码头上大喊起来，嚷着说她听到有船过来。我们压根没多想，以为自己与来的船不在一边。可噪声忽然大起来，大得盖住了我们踢水的声音。我们慌张失措起来。

我们朝码头喊回去，问他们是否看见有船，但没人看到。于是我们继续前进，船的轰鸣逐渐大得超过我们的声音。而后卡丽突然尖声叫道："回来!"她的声音里充满恐惧，所以我们紧张地搜索着船的踪影。卡丽正对着引擎轰鸣声处和我们脚踢着水的地方大喊起来："啊，天啊，船在那儿!"她说话的样子把我吓得魂不附体，我于是大哭起来。人人都没了主意。

我们尽量不乱动。切尔西和我都趴在气胎上，她在我左边，保罗在我右边，浮在水里。一停下来，我只听到自己的心脏狂跳不已，四周的叫喊声此起彼落，每过一秒船声就越近。接着，突然就在我前方出现了我最惊怕的噩梦。一艘船就在几英尺开外，它正朝我们驶来！

切尔西僵在原处惊叫着。我把她推入水里并随后也扎了进去，差点自己就没命了。我潜到水底，感觉到船像只喷气机般从肩头碾过。

我在水里抬起头，一时找不着水面。后来还是浮了出来，深深地大呼一口气。但险境尚未结束。船为了检查刚才撞到什么又开了回来，差点再次撞着我们。

我露出水面时切尔西已出来了，我听到她在呼喊着保罗和我。我答应了她，可保罗没有动静。当时好像是喊了保罗很久，但现在回想起来，只有20秒。保罗终于从水里钻出来，我们朝码头游去。卡丽是用救生绳把我从水里拖出来的，因为我那时已经无法动弹了。等我们全都上了码头后，船上的一个人帮我们把气胎拉回来。

保罗不停地自责，说他差点害了大家。我们安慰他说，决定是一起作出的，不能怪他。我们坐在码头上讲述刚才各自的经历。3人故事的不同之处在于被船撞到的位置不一样。船在我努力避开船底的时候撞着了我的肩膀。切尔西是用双手推开船的，保罗被撞着的是头。人人都认为我把切尔西从气胎上推下去是救了她一命。

第二天正是父亲节，下午，父母和我到保罗家去一起外出会餐。我们在码头上坐下后，我们跟他们讲述了那番经历。那天很长的时间里我一直在想，我们能活下来真是太幸运了。那次事件在随后将近一年的时间里让我恶梦频频。时至今日我还能看见水波的颜色，能感到露出水面时的心跳。我将永远铭记那次经历。

确凿无疑的是，下次我们再在晚上游湖，一定会带盏灯！

Daddy's Little Girl

爸爸的小女儿

Michele Campbell

迈克尔·卡贝尔

"Will you tell Daddy for me?"

That was the worst part. At seventeen, telling my mom I was pregnant was hard enough, but telling my dad was impossible. Daddy had always been a constant source of courage in my life. He had always looked at me with pride, and I had always tried to live my life in a way that would make him proud. Until this. Now it would all be shattered. I would no longer be Daddy's little girl. He would never look at me the same again. I heaved a defeated sigh and leaned against my mom for comfort.

"I'll have to take you somewhere while I tell your father. Do you understand why?"

"Yes, Mama." Because he wouldn't be able to look at me, that's why.

I went to spend the evening with the minister of our church, Brother Lu, who was the only person I felt comfortable with at that time. He counseled and consoled me, while Mom went home and called my dad at work to break the news.

It was all so unreal. At that time, being with someone who didn't judge me was a good thing. We prayed and talked, and I began to accept and understand the road that lay ahead for me. Then I saw the headlights in the window.

Mom had come back to take me home, and I knew Dad would be with her. I was so afraid. I ran out of the living room and into the small bathroom, closing and locking the door. Brother Lu followed and gently reprimanded me.

"Missy, you can't do this. You have to face him sooner or later. He isn't going home without you. Come on."

"Okay, but will you stay with me? I'm scared."

"Of course, Missy. Of course." I opened the door and slowly followed Brother Lu back to the living room. Mom and Dad still hadn't come in yet. I figured they were sitting in the car, preparing Dad for what to do or say when he saw me. Mom knew how afraid I was. But it wasn't fear that my father would yell at me or be angry with me. I wasn't afraid of him. It was the sadness in his eyes that frightened me. I had been in trouble and pain, and had not come to him for help and support. The realization that I was no longer his little girl.

I heard the footsteps on the sidewalk and the light tap on the wooden door. My lip began to quiver, opening a new floodgate of tears, and I hid behind Brother Lu. Mom walked in first and hugged him, then looked at me with a weak smile. Her eyes were swollen from her own tears, and I was thankful she had not wept in front of me. And then he was there. He didn't even shake Luther's hand, just nodded as he swept by, coming to me and gathering me up into his strong arms, holding me close as he whispered to me, "I love you. I love you, and I will love your baby, too."

He didn't cry. Not my dad. But I felt him quiver against me. I knew it took all of his control not to cry, and I was proud of him for that. And thankful. When he pulled back and looked at me, there was love and pride in his eyes. Even at that difficult moment.

"I'm sorry, Daddy. I love you so much."

"I know. Let's go home." And home we went. All of my fear was gone. There would still be pain and trials that I could not even imagine. But I had a strong, loving family that I knew would always be there for me. Most of all, I was still Daddy's little girl, and armed with that knowledge, there wasn't a mountain I couldn't climb or a storm I couldn't weather.

Thank you, Daddy.

"您会替我告诉爸爸吗?"

这是最糟糕的时候。17 岁的时候告诉妈妈我怀孕了已经是很困难了，但要告诉爸爸简直就是不可能的事。在我生命中爸爸一直不断地鼓励着我。他总是充满自豪地看着我，而我也努力使我的生命能够让他值得骄傲。直到这件事情发生了。一切都完了。我不再是爸爸的小女孩儿了。他不会再那样满带自豪地看着我。我长长地叹了口气，好像被打败了一样，然后靠在妈妈的身上以寻求慰藉。

"我跟你爸说的时候我得把你带到其他地方去。你知道为什么吗?"

"是的，妈妈。"因为他绝不能看到我这个样子，这就是原因。

那天晚上我去我们教堂的牧师 Brother Lu 家借宿，他是那个时候我唯一感到能够舒服地呆在一起的人。他和我谈话，安慰我，而此时妈妈回家，给正在工作的爸爸打去电话告诉了他这件事情。

一切都是那么不真实。在那个时候，和一个不对我评头论足的人在一起是很好的。我们一起祈祷和交谈，我开始接受并且明白自己面前的路。然后我看到窗外的车头灯了。

妈妈来接我回家了。我知道爸爸和她在一起。我害怕极了。我跑出起居室，躲在了狭小的洗手间里，锁上了门。Brother Lu 跟了过来，轻轻地申斥我。

"小姑娘，别这样。你迟早是要面对他的。没有你他是不会回家的。来吧。"

"好吧，但是你会和我在一起吗？我很害怕。"

"当然，小姑娘，当然。"我慢慢地打开门，跟着 Brother Lu 回到起居室。妈妈和爸爸还没有进来。我想他们是在车里等我，告诉爸爸看到我的时候该说什么做什么。妈妈知道我有多么害怕。但我并不是怕他骂我或是生我的气。我不怕他，只是他眼中的哀伤使我感到恐惧。我有麻烦，受到伤害，但是却没有向他寻求帮助和支持。也意识到自己不再是他的小女孩儿了。

我听到人行道上的脚步声，以及轻轻叩门的声音。我的嘴唇开始轻轻颤抖，泪水抑制不住地开始往下流。我躲在了 Brother Lu 背后。妈妈第一个进来，和他拥抱了一下，然后对着我勉强笑了笑。她的眼睛里噙着泪水，我很感激她没有在我面前哭出来。然后爸爸来了。他甚至没有和 Luther 握手，只是走过时点了点头。他径直走到我面前，用他有力的臂膀把我抱了起来，紧紧地，向我耳语道："我爱你，我爱你，我也会爱你的小宝贝的。"

他没有哭。爸爸不会哭，但是我感到他在颤抖。我知道他用尽了全身力气让自己不哭出来，对此我相当自豪，也相当感激。当他抬起头来再看着我时，他的眼中充满爱与自豪，即使在困难的时候。

"对不起，爸爸。我太爱你了。"

"我知道，我们回家吧。"于是我们回家了。我的泪水消失得无影无踪。以后可能仍然会有我无法想象的伤害和试炼。但是我有一个坚强的、充满爱心的家庭，我知道他们会一直支持我。最重要的是，我仍然是爸爸的小女孩儿，只要知道这一点，我就可以跨越一切艰难险阻。

谢谢你，爸爸。

Grandfather's Clock

祖父的大钟

Kathy Fasiq

凯西·凡希

In the dining room of my grandfather's house stood a massive grandfather clock. Meals in that dining room were a time for four generations to become one. The table was always spread with food from wonderful family recipes all containing love as the main ingredient. And always that grandfather clock stood like a trusted old family friend, watching over the laughter and story swapping and gentle kidding that were a part of our lives.

As a child, the old clock fascinated me. I watched and listened to it during meals. I marveled at how at different times of the day, that clock would chime three times, six times or more, with a wonderful resonant sound that echoed throughout the house. I found the clock comforting. Familiar. Year after year, the clock chimed, a part of my memories, a part of my heart.

在我祖父的餐厅里有一座巨大的座钟。每天在餐厅吃饭的时候，我们家四代人就待在一起。餐桌上的食物都是精致的家庭菜肴，包含着家庭的爱。那座大钟总是站在那里，像一个信任的家庭老朋友，看着我们笑，讲故事和开玩笑。这已经成了我们生活的一部分了。

作为一个孩子，这钟使我着迷。吃饭的时候我看着它，倾听它。我总是觉得每天不同的时候钟会敲三下，六下，或者更多，而且那还带着相当美妙的声响，在整个屋子里回荡。我感到这座钟相当令人安心，熟悉。年复一年，钟响不断，成了我记忆的一部分，我心的一部分。

Even more wonderful to me was my grandfather's ritual. He meticulously wound that clock with a special key each day. That key was magic to me. It kept our family's magnificent clock ticking and chiming, a part of every holiday and every tradition, as solid as the wood from which it was made. I remember watching as my grand-father took the key from his pocket and opened the hidden door in the massive old clock. He inserted the key and wound — not too much, never overwind, he'd tell me solemnly. Nor too little. He never let that clock wind down and stop. When we grandkids got a little older, he showed us how to open the door to the grandfather clock and let us each take a turn winding the key. I remember the first time I did, I trembled with anticipation. To be part of this family ritual was sacred.

After my beloved grandfather died, it was several days after the funeral before I remembered the clock!

"Mama! The clock! We've let it wind down."

对我来说更精彩的是祖父的“典礼”。他每天小心翼翼地用一把特殊的钥匙给钟上发条。那钥匙对我来说有一种魔力。它让我们家高大的钟嘀嗒嘀嗒走和报时，这是每个假期每个传统的一部分，就像造这座钟的木头一样坚固不变。我记得看着祖父从兜里掏出钥匙，打开这座大钟的隐藏的门。他插入钥匙，然后开始转——“不要太多，绝对不要上过头”，他会严肃地告诉我。也不要太少。他从没有让钟停止工作过。当我们这些孙辈长大了一些之后，他教我们如何打开老钟的门，然后让我们每人去转一圈钥匙。我记得第一次做的时候，稍稍有些预知的颤抖。成为这个家庭典礼的一部分是神圣的。

在我深爱的祖父过世之后，直到葬礼过后几天我才记起那座钟！

“妈妈！钟！它停了！”

The tears flowed freely when I entered the dining room. The clock stood forlornly quiet. As quiet as the funeral parlor had been. Hushed. The clock even seemed smaller. Not quite as magnificent without my grandfather's special touch. I couldn't bear to look at it.

Sometime later, years later, my grandmother gave me the clock and the key. The old house was quiet. No bowls clanging, no laughter over the dinner table, no ticking or chiming of the clock — all was still. The hands on the clock were frozen, a reminder of time slipping away, stopped at the precise moment when my grandfather had ceased winding it. I took the key in my shaking hand and opened the clock door. All of a sudden, I was a child again, watching my grandfather with his silver-white hair and twinkling blue eyes. He was there, winking at me, at the secret of the clock's magic, at the key that held so much power. I stood, lost in the moment for a long time. Then slowly, reverently, I inserted the key and wound the clock. It sprang to life. Tick-tock, tick-tock, life and chimes were breathed into the dining room, into the house and into my heart. In the movement of the hands of the clock, my grandfather lived again.

我踏进餐厅的时候眼泪肆意地流淌下来。座钟静静地站在那里，被遗弃的，就如同葬礼的会客室那样安静。钟显得愈发小了。没了祖父特殊的抚摸，它变得光辉不再。我甚至不忍看它一眼。

一段时候之后，几年之后，我的祖母把钟和钥匙给了我。旧房子里一片静悄悄。没有球滚动的声响，没有餐桌旁的笑声，没有钟的嘀嗒声和报时声——一切都是静止的。扶在钟上的手如冻结了一般，时间的提示渐渐溜走，准确地停在祖父停止给它上发条的时候。我把钥匙拿在有些颤抖的手中，打开了钟的门。突然之间，我又变成了孩子，看着我的祖父，他那银白的头发和闪亮的蓝色眸子。他就在那里，注视着我，注视着座钟的魔法的秘密，注视着那把拥有无限力量的钥匙。我立在那里，久久地沉思。然后慢慢地，虔诚地，我插入了钥匙，开始给钟上发条。它又回复了生机。嘀嗒，嘀嗒，整个餐厅，整个房子，还有我的心，都被注入了活力。就在座钟走的时候，祖父又一次活在了这里。

Grandpa's Bee

祖父的蜜蜂

Anonymous/佚名

A long time before I was born, my Grandma and Grandpa moved into the house on Beechwood Avenue. They had a young family — of 4 little girls. The little girls Slept in the attic in a big feather bed. It was cold there on winter night. Grandma put hot bricks under the covers at the foot of the bed to keep the little girls warm.

During the Great Depression, work was hard to find, so Grandpa did whatever jobs he could. He dug ditches during the week and on Weekend he and Grandma dug a garden to grow some of their own food.

早在我出生以前，奶奶和爷爷搬到碧奇乌大道住。他们膝下养有4个小女儿。女孩们睡在阁楼的一张大羽毛床上。那里冬夜酷寒。奶奶得在床脚下垫热砖给女儿们取暖。

大萧条时期，工作很难找，爷爷什么苦工都做。平时他挖沟渠，周末和奶奶在花园里挖挖锄锄，种点自己的口粮。

The house on Beechwood Avenue had a big Front yard with shade trees and fruit trees. In the middle of the yard was a water pump where the four little girls pumped water for cooking, cleaning and watering the garden. On one side of the yard, grandma and grandpa planted tomatoes, beans, squash, cucumbers, peppers and strawberries to feed their growing family. They planted roses geraniums lilacs and irises on the other Side of the yard, around the statue of the Blessed Mother.

Everybody worked to keep the garden growing. All summer long, the family ate food from the garden and enjoyed the beautiful flowers. Grandma put up strawberry jam, tomatoes, beans, peppers, pears and peaches in canning jam. They were good to eat through the long winter.

The family grew up, and before too many years had passed, the grandchildren came to visit. Grandma and Grandpa still planted their garden every spring. Everyone still enjoyed the good food from the garden and always took some home.

碧奇乌大道的房子有个大前院，院子里种着浓荫遮蔽的大树和果树。院中央的是个水泵，小女孩们就在这里用泵水来做饭、打扫卫生、灌溉花园。奶奶和爷爷在院子的一边种上番茄、豆子、南瓜、黄瓜、辣椒和草莓，供应这个大家庭的吃用。在另一边，他们围着圣母的雕像种了玫瑰、天竺葵、丁香和蝴蝶花。

人人都辛勤地耕种花园，使它日渐丰实。整个夏天，我们一家人吃着在花园中种出的食物，欣赏着花园里的美丽花朵。奶奶还把做好的草莓酱、番茄、豆子、辣椒、梨子和桃子装进罐子里，使它们的美味能保持一整个漫长的冬天。

多年过去，孩子们长大了，子孙们也来到了世上。奶奶和爷爷仍然每年春天都耕种花园。人人都能分享花园种出的好东西，也总能带上一些回家里。

Grandchildren grow up, and grandparents grow older. It became harder for Grandma and Grandpa to keep up the garden. So they made it a little smaller. There was still plenty to eat from the garden and lovely flowers to enjoy.

Then one summer when Grandpa was eighty-nine years old, all he could do was watch from his lawn chair as the vegetables grew and the roses bloomed. Summer slowly faded, and Grandpa died before it was time to bring in the harvest.

It was a lonely winter for Grandma. She sat near the window, looking out at the yard and wondering if she could plant the garden in the spring. It would be hard to care for it by herself. When spring came, she planted only a little garden.

One sunny day in the early summer, Grandma heard a commotion in the front yard and looked out the window to see a frightening sight a gigantic swarm of bees filled the air between two tall trees. There were thousands of bees in the air, so many that the swarm reached the tree-tops! The buzzing sound was tremendous. Grandma watched as the bees made their way into a hole up in one of the trees. Before long, every one of those bees had disappeared into its new home.

孙子孙女们长大了，爷爷、奶奶年迈古稀。维护花园对他们来说有些难度了，所以他们缩小了些花园的面积。但里面种出来的食物还足够吃，花朵也还招人喜爱。

等到爷爷89岁的那个夏天，他只能坐在草地的椅子上，看蔬菜长大，玫瑰开花。夏日渐渐消逝，爷爷在丰收前就去世了。

对奶奶来说，这是个寂寞的冬天。她坐在窗边，望着外边的院子，考虑着来年春天还要不要耕种花园。只靠她自己来打理太难了些。当春天来到时，她只稍微种了一点。

初夏的一天，阳光灿烂，奶奶听到前院传来一阵骚动声，她向窗外望去，看到震撼的一幕。两棵大树上满满缀着大团大团的蜜蜂。空中还飞舞着成千上万只，多不胜数的蜂群一直排到树梢上！嗡嗡声不绝于耳。奶奶看见这些蜜蜂先后钻进一棵树上高高的树洞中。很快，所有的蜜蜂都搬进新家，消失了。

Grandma wondered what in the world she could do. Should she hair someone to get rid of bees? That would cost more than she could afford. She decided to wait and think it over.

During the next few days, the bees were busy making their own business. Grandma could always see a few bees buzzing in and out around the opening high in the tree. Before long, she decided the bees won't bother anyone, so she went about her business and didn't give them any other thought.

That summer, Grandma's little garden grew and grew. The neighbors would stop to admire the huge crop of vegetables and puzzle over their own gardens weren't doing well. No matter, because Grandma had enough give some away. Of course, everyone who came to visit was treated to a meal of good things from the garden.

One day, Grandma's brother Frank visited from Arizona. As Grandma made Frank a delicious lunch of squash pan cakes and home made apple sauce, she told him the story about the swam of bees.

Frank said, "in Arizona, the farmers often hired beekeepers to set up beehives near their fields. The bees pollinated the crops and helped them to grow."

That was when Grandma realized that her bees had helped with her garden all summer.

"So that's why my little garden had such a big crop!" she exclaimed.

From that Time on, Grandma always believed that since Grandpa couldn't be there to help her that summer, he had sent the bees to take his place and make Grandma's little garden grow and grow...

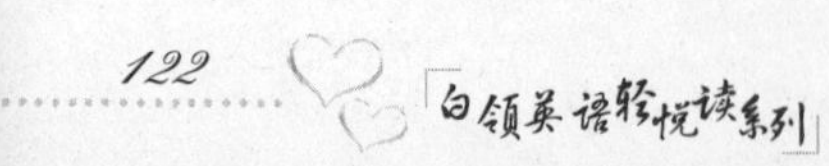

奶奶不禁发愁起来。她是否该请人清走这些蜜蜂呢？但是她根本支付不起费用。于是她决定等一等，再想想办法。

随后几天，蜜蜂忙碌个不停。奶奶总能看到有一些蜂儿从高高的树洞里嗡嗡地飞进飞出。不久，她看出蜜蜂并无妨碍，于是自顾自地干活，不再理会它们。

那年夏天，奶奶的小花园硕果累累。邻居们都驻足羡慕里面生长的丰盛的蔬菜，纳罕怎么自己花园中作物的长势就没有这么喜人。没关系，因为奶奶有好多可以送人。登门来访的人当然都有花园里的美味来招待。

一天，奶奶的弟弟法兰克从亚利桑那州前来拜访。奶奶给他做了一顿香喷喷的午饭，有南瓜饼，有自制的苹果酱，她还把蜜蜂的故事告诉了法兰克。

法兰克说：“在亚利桑那，农夫们常常雇请养蜂人在农田附近搭蜂箱。蜜蜂授粉有助于庄稼成长。”

奶奶才意识到，原来是这些蜜蜂在夏季助成了花园的丰收。

“所以我的小花园才有了大丰收！”她大声地说道。

从那时开始，奶奶便相信是因为爷爷那年夏天没能亲自帮她，才派了蜜蜂到这里，让奶奶的小花园欣欣向荣。

Our House

我们的家

Edgar Guest

埃德加·格斯特

We play at our house and have all sorts of fun,
An' there's always a game when supper is done;
An' at our house there's marks on the walls an' the stairs,
An' some terrible scratches on some of the chairs;
An' ma says that our house is surely a fright,
But pa and I say that our house is all right.

At our house we laugh an' we sing an' we shout,
An' whirl all the chairs and the tables about,
An' I rassle my pa an' I get him down too,
An' he's all out of breath when the fightin' is through;
Am' ma says our house is surely a sight,
But pa an' I say that our house is all right.

I've been to houses with pa where I had
To sit in a chair like a good little lad,
An' there wasn't a mark on the walls an' the chairs,
An' the stuff that we have couldn't come up to theirs;
An' pa said to ma that for all of their joy
He wouldn't change places and give up his boy.

在家里玩，我们乐趣无穷，
晚饭做好时，总会还有一个游戏；
墙上楼梯上都是印记，
有些椅子上还有可怕的抓痕；
妈妈说我们的家绝对是一个令人惊讶的地方，
但爸爸和我说这里一切都好。

在家里我们大笑，我们唱歌，我们喊叫，
围着桌椅四处乱跳，
我和爸爸摔跤，也还赢了他，
打闹结束时，他已经气喘吁吁了。
妈妈说我们的家绝对是一个值得观赏的地方，
但爸爸和我说这里一切都好。

我和爸爸去过好多房子，
那里我都必须得像个好孩子，乖乖坐在椅子上。
墙上和椅子上都没有印记，
我们有的东西不可能在这里发生；
爸爸对妈妈说因为这有他们所有的快乐，
他不会换地方和放弃他的孩子。

They never have races nor rassles nor fights.

Coz they have no children to play with at nights;

An' their walls are all clean and their curtains hang straight,

An' everthing's shiny an' right up to date;

But pa says with all of its racket an' fuss,

He'd rather by far live at our house with us.

他们从来没有比赛，没有摔跤，没有打闹。

因为晚上没有孩子和他们一起玩；

墙都很干净，窗帘拉得很直，

器物闪闪发光，新潮而时尚；

但是爸爸说就算是这些喧闹和惊异，

他都愿意和我们一直住在我们的家里。

The Big Screen

大屏幕

Linda Ferris

琳达·费里斯

I was the oldest of five children back in the 60's. We lived in a nice little three bedroom bungalow in Lincoln Park, Michigan. Mom and Dad worked so hard, yet always found the time to spend with us. My mother always laughed when she said "we were an especially active bunch" and the only place they could take five active children back then, where they could also find time to be alone, was the "drive-in" movies!

We always looked forward to going to the drive-in! Mom would fill a big brown grocery bag, with homemade, hot buttered, popcorn. We would put our pajamas on underneath our clothing, gather our pillows and blankets, hop into our nine passenger station wagon, and off we'd go.

60 年代时，我是家里 5 个孩子中最大的。我们住在密歇根林肯公园一处很小但是很舒适的三居室的平房里。父母工作都十分努力，但他们总是可以找到时间和我们呆在一起。妈妈在说到“我们是一帮特别活跃的人”时，总会哈哈大笑。唯一一个能让 5 个活跃的孩子在一起，也能让他们找到独处时间的地方，就是汽车电影院。

我们总是期盼着去汽车电影院！妈妈会用一个大的褐色购物袋装满自家做的热乎乎带着奶油的爆米花。我们会在外套下穿上睡衣，带上枕头和毯子，跳进我们能坐 9 人的客货两用车，然后就出发了。

On the way there, Dad would make a special stop at the penny candy store, where we were all allowed to fill a little brown bag with all kinds of penny candy. We were so excited, as we carried our treasures back to the car, knowing we couldn't eat it until the cartoon began.

We would get there early, so that we could play on the playground, right under the BIG screen — all the time having great anticipation for the movie projector lights to flash on. We kept a constant watch.

As soon as it started to get dark, the screen lit up, and we would race back to the car, tearing off our outer clothing right down to our pajamas. The car was filled with commotion, as we giggled and squirmed, filling our bellies with candy and popcorn.

There were always two cartoons playing before the movie back then, great ones, like Felix the Cat, The Coyote, and Tom and Jerry. But what was just as exciting was the ticking clock advertisement for the refreshment stand, with dancing hot dogs, candy and ice cream. That came on right before the movie. It was all that five rambunctious kids could hope for, and by then, stay awake for.

去那儿的路上，爸爸通常会在一便士糖果店那里特地停一下，他允许我们在那儿可以用任何的一便士糖果把一个小的褐色袋子装满。我们都相当兴奋，把这些“珍宝”带回车里，知道在动画片开始之前我们不会吃的。

通常我们会早到一些，因此我们可以在场地上玩会儿，就在那个大屏幕下面。我们一直也都期待着投影机的灯会突然一下亮起来，于是时不时地都会关心地看看。

天一黑，屏幕就点亮了，我们就跑回车里，脱掉外套，就剩下睡衣。我们嘻嘻哈哈，互相打闹，车里一片骚动，还不停地吃着糖果和爆米花。

那时在电影开始之前，总会放两部动画片，很有名的那种，比如说《菲立克斯猫》，《The Coyote》和《猫和老鼠》。同样激动人心的是那个嘀嗒钟的快餐店广告：有跳舞的热狗、糖果和冰淇淋。这个就在电影开始前放映。这是那5个难以控制的孩子所能期盼的全部，也是之后保持清醒的动力。

Yeah, Mom and Dad were pretty clever. For they now had five children all in their pajamas, exhausted from playing in the night air, appetites satisfied, and fast asleep BEFORE the two feature films were even showing.

As I got a little older I would watch a little of the movie before giving in to sleep. And as the others slept, I felt comfort in watching Mom and Dad, as they looked at each other and smiled, his arm around her, enjoying the peace and quiet.

We would get home around 2 a. m. — pretty late for us — as Mom helped us drag ourselves and our pillows to our beds and as dad carried in the little ones.

I was disappointed the day they closed the last drive-in in our town.

It will always hold special memories for us — those days of penny candy, pajamas under our clothes and station wagons.

是啊，妈妈和爸爸都相当聪明。他们的5个孩子都穿着睡衣，玩了一晚上也累了，吃得饱饱的，在电影正式开始之前就已经沉沉入睡了。

当我长大一点之后，我会在睡觉前看一点点电影。其他人都睡着之后，看着妈妈和爸爸我感到很温馨，因为他们互相看着对方，微笑，他抱着她，享受这平和与宁静。

我们一般在凌晨2点回家——对我们来说相当晚了——妈妈帮着我们把我们自己和我们的枕头挪到床上，而爸爸就抱着小一些的。

镇里最后一家汽车电影院关闭的时候，我感到很失望。

它对我们来说意味着特殊的记忆——那些有一便士糖果，外衣下的睡衣和客货两用车的日子。

F-A-M-I-L-Y
家

Anonymous/佚名

I ran into a stranger as he passed by.
"Oh, excuse me please" was my reply.
He said, "Please excuse me too;
I wasn't even watching for you."
We were very polite, this stranger and I.
We went on our way and we said good-bye.

But at home a different story is told,
how we treat our loved ones, young and old.
Later that day, cooking the evening meal,
my daughter stood beside me very still.
When I turned, I nearly knocked her down.
"Move out of the way," I said with a frown.

我撞到了一个路过的陌生人。
“噢，请原谅我。”我说道。
他说：“也请原谅我；
我甚至没有看到你。”
我们都很礼貌，这个陌生人和我。
我们走上各自的路，然后互道再见。

但在家里却是另一个故事，
我们怎样对待我们爱的人，不论老幼。
那天晚些时候，我在做晚饭，
我女儿静静地站在我旁边。
我转身时差点把她撞倒。
“别挡道！”我皱着眉头说道。

She walked away, her little heart broken.
I didn't realize how harshly I'd spoken.
While I lay awake in bed,
God's still small voice came to me and said,
"While dealing with a stranger…
common courtesy you use,
but the children you love,
you seem to abuse.

Look on the kitchen floor;
you'll find some flowers there by the door.
Those are the flowers she brought for you.
She picked them herself, pink, yellow and blue.
She stood quietly not to spoil the surprise,
and you never saw the tears in her eyes."

她走开了，小小的心受到了伤害。
我没有意识到我说了多么严厉的话。
当我在床上久久不能入睡时，
上帝沉稳而低细的声音传到了我的耳中，
"对待陌生人时，
你可以彬彬有礼，
但是对你爱的孩子，
你却粗暴无礼。

看看厨房的地板；
你会在门边找到一些花朵。
那些是她带来给你的花。
她自己摘的，粉色，黄色和蓝色。
她静静地站在那里，只是不想破坏这份惊喜，
而且你从未看到她眼里噙着的泪水。"

By this time, I felt very small
and now my tears began to fall.
I quietly went and knelt by her bed;
"Wake up, little girl, wake up," I said.
"Are these the flowers you picked for me?"
She smiled, "I found 'em, out by the tree.
I picked 'em because they're pretty like you.

I knew you'd like 'em, especially the blue."
I said, "Daughter, I'm sorry for the way I acted today;
I shouldn't have yelled at you that way."
She said, "Oh, Mom, that's okay.
I love you anyway."
I said, "Daughter, I love you too,
and I do like the flowers,
especially the blue."

这一刻我感到自己十分渺小，
我的眼泪开始流下。
我悄悄走了过去，在她床边跪下：
"醒醒，小女孩儿，醒醒。"我说道。
"这些是你为我摘的花吗?"
她微笑道，"我在树边找到的。
我摘了下来，因为它们很像你。

我知道你会喜欢它们，尤其是蓝色的。"
我说道："女儿，我对我今天做的感到很抱歉；
我不应该冲你大吼大叫。"
她说"噢，妈妈，没事儿。
不管怎么样我都爱你。"
我说道："我也爱你，女儿，
我很喜欢这些花，
尤其是蓝色的花。"

Are you aware that: If we die tomorrow, the company that we are working for could easily replace us in a matter of days. But the family we left behind will feel the loss for the rest of their lives. And come to think of it, we pour ourselves more into work than to our family — an unwise investment indeed. So what is moral to the story?
Do you know what the word "FAMILY" stands for?

FAMILY = (F) ather (A) nd (M) other, (I) (L) ove (Y) ou!

你知道吗？如果我们明天就死了，我们工作的
公司用不了几天就能找人来替代我们。
但是我们留下的家庭却会在他们剩下的生命中
感到悲伤。仔细想想，我们更多地
把自己投入到了工作而不是家庭中——一个不明智
选择。那么这个故事想要说什么呢？
你知道"FAMILY"这个单词代表什么吗？

FAMILY = (F) ather (A) nd (M) other, (I) (L) ove (Y) ou!

The Choice

选择

Theodore A. Yulo, Jr 西奥多·嘉诺

"Your wife has suffered abruptio-placenta. The baby is now on its eight month but he's in distress; his heart is beating faster than that of a running dog's. You will have to make a choice, sir. Shall we try to save your wife or your child?"

I struggled to assimilate the doctor's words as I ran my sweaty palms over my hair. Was she asking me which of the two I had to give up? I didn't have an answer. I had read somewhere what they would have to do with the child should I tell them to save my wife. It was unthinkable?

Silently, I shook my head. The doctor compassionately nodded her head and said, "This is difficult, I know. Please take all the time you need to think. You may want to tell your wife about our dilemma."

"你妻子现在胎盘分离了。婴儿现在有8个月了，但是他很危险；他的心跳速度比一只奔跑的狗还快。你得选择一下，先生。我们应该救您的妻子还是孩子?"

我一边用汗湿的手理着头发，一边挣扎着理解医生的话。她在问我这两者之间我不得不放弃哪一个吗? 我没有答案。我知道如果我让他们救我妻子的话他们会对我的孩子做什么。这是不可想象的事。

静静地，我摇了摇头。医生同情地点点头说道："这很困难，我知道。请尽量好好考虑吧，您可能想要告诉您妻子我们现在的处境。"

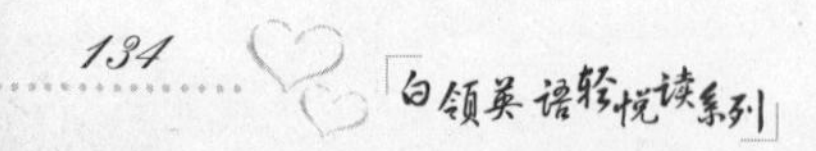

I entered my wife's room and sat beside her. She was breathing heavily and pain lined her brows severely. "What's wrong?" she said breathlessly.

"They say I have to choose between you and our child. I choose both of you, not either one of you." I cried.

"Save the child, sweetheart. And when I'm gone, promise to take care of the baby and our four other girls. I'll be okay." my wife calmly said.

I shook my head again then, slowly turned away. There was only one other place to go now. I knelt on the pew of the vacant chapel and faced the cross. At the side, I could see the images of three Saints: Francis, Raymond, and Martin.

I bowed my head as my tears flowed, saying, "Lord, I may get the best doctor in the world for my wife and child but if I don't have Your Blessing, she will not be able to do anything for them. But I trust that You love me, that You love Teresita and the baby. Have mercy on us. I promise that though You may choose to take them both, I will still Love You."

我走进我妻子的病房，坐在她旁边。她呼吸很重，面部因为疼痛而显得有些扭曲。“怎么回事?”她有些有气无力地问道。

“他们说我必须在你和我们孩子之间作出选择。我要你们两个，而不只是其中一个。”我喊道。

“保住孩子吧，亲爱的。我走了之后，一定要照顾好孩子和我们其他4个女孩儿。我没事的。”她平静地说道。

我又一次摇了摇头，慢慢地扭了过去。现在只有一个地方可去了。我跪在空无一人的教堂里的长凳上，面对着十字架。在它旁边，我看到了三个圣徒的画像：弗兰西斯、雷蒙德和马丁。

我低下了头，泪水淌下，说到：“主啊，我可以为我的妻子和孩子找到世上最好的医生，但是如果没有您的佑护，医生就无能为力啊。但我相信您爱着我，爱着 Tersita 和孩子。发发慈悲吧，我发誓，即使您可能把他们两个都带走，我也仍然爱你。”

As I wept quietly, I seemed to see the Lord smiling down at me through my eyes of faith. He stretched out His hand and held my shoulder. I looked up then. I dried my tears, stood up, and left the chapel.

As I went to my wife's room, the doctor looked up expectantly. I smiled at her and said, "Just do the best you can."

Hours later, at 3: 00 a. m., an attendant came in and roused me from the restless doze I had fallen into. "Your wife has given birth!" she said excitedly.

"And the child?" I asked eagerly.

"It's a boy! You can see him at the nursery tomorrow. We have to warn you that he's in an incubator though."

I couldn't say a word. Tears of joy started to pour down on my cheek and once more, I fell on my knees saying, "Thank You, Father. Thank You."

Two months later, at my son's baptism, the priest asked me, "What shall we name the child?" I proudly answered, "Francis Raymond Martin, Father."

我静静地哭泣，似乎看到上帝对着我虔诚的眼睛微笑。他伸出他的手，抓住了我的肩膀。于是我抬起头来，擦去了眼泪，站起来，离开了教堂。

我走进妻子的病房，医生充满期待地望着我。我微笑着说道："请尽您最大努力就好了。"

几个小时之后，凌晨3点，一个护士走进来把我从瞌睡中惊醒。"您太太生了！"她兴奋地说道。

"孩子呢？"我急切地问道。

"是个男孩儿！明天您就可以在育婴室看到他了。不过我们得跟您说他还在保育器里。"

我一句话也说不出来。喜悦的泪水一次又一次地从我的脸颊上滑落，我跪下去说道："感谢上帝，感谢上帝。"

两个月后，我儿子洗礼时，牧师问我："您给孩子取什么名字？"我自豪地回答道："弗兰西斯·雷蒙德·马丁，先生。"

Home Truth

家的真相

Anonymous/佚名

It was the smell of rain that I missed the most and the sound of a lawnmower and the waft of cut grass. It was being out in the open and standing bare foot! Blue skies part and parcel of it all; the thunder that would blast over and leave — the coming of a tropical sundown, an evening of barbecues, of warm pools, beer splattering on concrete. The bed awaiting, a vest, a body glistening from perspiration and a sleep of pillows constantly changing sides, a mosquito in the ear. Sleepless nights that were all you knew. And then, one day I left it behind. I moved to a city, to grim faced pallid movements, and there I became with them a ghost on the sidewalks. Dimly, ambling along with my face down, watching my steps and hurrying towards my quotidian activities.

雨水的气息最让我怀念，还有割草机的声音和那扬起的草屑。赤足站在户外，头顶一片蓝天，雷声在头顶响起，然后逐渐远去——在热带地区的一个黄昏，一个烧烤的夜晚、在温暖的池塘边，啤酒洒落在水泥地上。静默的床、背心、汗湿的身体，辗转难眠，蚊子在耳边嗡鸣——一个个不眠之夜，那情景就像你所知道的那样。然后，突然有一天，我抛开了一切，移居到了城市，迎向毫无生气的城市生活，成为众多麻木的城里人的一员。我稀里糊涂地，每天低着头，盯着自己的脚步，日复一日地忙碌于生活。

Winters I spent indoor in solace. My flat mates — the friends I had — worked day and night. They were accustomed to leaving the soul behind, the need for money was so official. I would spend nights in the strange house, with creaks of a wall I did not know, and sit by the phone that our landlord had locked, and think of conversations of the past, of my mother's voice ringing, of my best friend whom I would lose contact with, and I would write letters, letters I would never send, letters that clutched the truth — that only I knew. I would cry, tears staining the ink, a smudged idea of love. I was then doing mindless data entry, tapping words into a computer, and moving on wondering what worth there was, and how to find it. My flat mates would come home just before midnight — Mark and Craig, my two best friends. I would smile inwardly and outwardly and make them tea, a sandwich, sit with them and live their lives, hear their stories, flourish in company. Sleep would be eschewed, I yearned for comfort, and company eased the etching of loneliness.

冬天，我独自躲在屋里。室友，也就是我的朋友们，每天从早忙到晚。他们习惯了没有思想，赚钱才是天经地义的事。我整夜整夜地一个人呆在这个陌生的屋子里，只有墙壁发出些莫名其妙的声音。我坐在被房东锁上了的电话机旁，回忆着过去的一些对话——那是妈妈的声音，还有已失去联络的好友说的话。我写信，写从来不寄出去的信，里面全是只有我才知道的真心话。我哭，泪水把字迹化掉，把爱念涂污。那时我正在打一份临时工，每天机械地把资料输入电脑，边打字边质疑着做这些工作的价值，以及如何才能实现它的价值。我的室友马克和克雷格——我最好的朋友，要到午夜时分才回来。我会带着满心的欢喜和满脸的笑容，帮他们泡茶、做三文治，和他们坐在一起，感受他们的生活，听他们的故事，和他们一起激动。睡眠也被省略掉了，我渴望安慰，和别人呆在一起才能缓和孤独的侵蚀。

I drank a lot, I had a job and I met people, and I continued my ambling in a city that was not mine. Every Friday my work offered free drinks and I catapulted towards the bar, I sipped ferociously at the wine, the beer, I got horrifically drunk and so the person that I was not, but so yearned to be would come out. She, loud, vivacious, articulate would spend the evening conversing with strangers, laughing and sometimes, flirting! I seemed to step out of myself and watch in amazement. After drinks, I would stumble to the Palladium to meet Mark and Craig — they both worked there as ushers. I would arrive as they were finishing work and we would sit in the bar and I would continue, I would drink.

One night we fell drunk into the house. I lit a cigarette; I sat down and my mind triggered off dull thuds of depression. I went to the bathroom and in a mode of translucent mania I took out a razor blade and in numb motions slowly cut at my wrist, tears streaming down my face, I stopped as soon as I started, my aim was wrong — it was in the name of attention, except I would tell nobody, the attention was all to myself. Quietly, I wrapped my stinging arm with toilet paper, walked to my room and put on a jersey so as to cover the threat, the childish self abuse. I lay and quickly wiped my tears as I heard the friendly footsteps of Mark and Craig. They stood and bantered and eventually I followed them downstairs, and listened to Bob Marley, and Redemption song, my favorite song — "Sold I to the merchant ships".

And so, I stood on the tube, Dollis Hill to Marylebone and I stared at the scars on my wrist. The scars of stupidity that only I knew of, I was entranced, as though it were not me — it's never me. I swayed to the motion of the train, the city was corrupting me, my soul was slowly bitten, I wanted to yell out my mind, but it all seeped inwards, I was boring myself with my own pleas.

我喝很多酒，有一份工作，结交朋友，并且继续在一个不属于我的城市里游荡。每逢星期五，我都可以因工作之便享受免费的酒水。那时，我总是像一支离弦箭似地冲去酒吧，大口大口地喝着各种各样的酒，直到酩酊大醉。这样，我才能展现出我的另一面，做我渴望做而又不能做的事——这个她，说话响亮、活泼好动、伶牙俐齿，整晚和陌生人说说笑笑，有时甚至跟他们调情。我仿佛脱离了自己，惊讶地旁观着这一切。喝了一通后，我会踉踉跄跄地到帕拉狄昂剧院与马克和克雷格碰头，他们两人都在那里当引座员。我通常在他们临近下班的时候到那儿，然后我们就一起去酒吧，我呢，就继续喝酒。

有一天晚上我们跌跌撞撞地回到住所。我点燃一支香烟；坐了下来，脑子里突然充斥着抑郁的感觉。我走进浴室，在迷迷糊糊的烦躁状态下，我拿起剃刀片，麻木而缓慢地朝自己的手腕割下去。泪水顺着我的脸庞流下来，但刚一割下去我就停住了，我的目的是错的——我想引起注意，除非我不告诉别人，就只有我自己会注意到。我静静地用纸巾包好刺痛的手臂，回到房间，穿上运动衣盖住那吓人的伤口，那孩子气地自虐所带来的伤口。我躺了下来。听到马克和克雷格那熟悉的脚步声，我就迅速地擦干眼泪。他们站在我跟前，逗我笑，最后我跟着他们到楼下听鲍博·马利的《救赎歌》，我最爱的一首歌——“把我卖到商船上……”

就这样，我站在从多利斯山开往玛丽莱宝的地铁上，凝视着手腕上的伤疤。这是象征着愚蠢的伤疤，只有我才知道。我恍恍惚惚，仿佛我已不是我——不可能是我。我的身体随着列车摇动，这座城市让我渐渐沦落，我的灵魂逐渐地被吞噬，我希望把我的想法喊出来，但它却全部都潜藏在我心里，连我自己都对自己的渴求产生了厌倦。

It got better, as it does get better, as you know no better and I sunk into my life, I slowly enjoyed its offerings, I adjusted to the climate, to the people and one day as I walked outside my new flat — not mine of course, but my temporary abode that I rented, as I took out the garbage on a autumn Saturday — in my pajamas, with the TV and the glow of comfort, I looked at the grey, I sucked it in and I quite enjoyed it — it's romantic quality, it's gloom appealed to me, as it would eventually with my nature. I liked it. I went inside, and shivered — a content chill, I enjoyed the cold and the idea of being able to get warm and I lay on the couch with my toes under a cushion, an inane program keeping me entertained. It all grows on you.

后来，情况有了改善，好像注定会有所改善似的；但在外人看来，我并没什么变化。我融入了自己的生活，我慢慢地开始享受生活所给予我的东西，我适应了这里的气候、这里的人，直至有一天我走出新的公寓——当然，那公寓并不属于我，而是我租来的临时栖身之所，当我在那个秋日的星期六，走出门外倒垃圾时——当时我穿着睡衣，屋里电视机开着，我感到舒适自在。我看着灰色的天空，吸了口气，挺享受的——是这种浪漫、阴郁吸引了我，因为我本性如此。我喜欢这样的感觉。我回到屋子里，身体在颤抖——一种让我心满意足的寒意。我喜欢感到寒冷，并喜欢知道自己能够取暖的感觉。我躺在沙发上，脚趾缩在软垫下面，一个无聊的电视节目也能让我觉得开心。我已经完全习惯了这样的生活。

I went home, eventually. I spent five months appreciating the beauty, the climate, the content natures surrounding me. I ate healthy food, I listened to a language I had forgotten about, I roamed on farms that were not mine, went to wine harvests, put on high factors to shield out the sun, spend days lamenting the heat. But, it was not time, I was unable to indulge as the city, London, was still with me, my love and loathing relationship was still continuing, I was still meant to be there, whether unhappy or not. I could not explain it, it's not the city I suppose, it's me — I need to be content. I left, I left what I love so much, no great epiphany, just not at that moment. One day home will come to me, or I will go to home and I await the knowledge in peace.

终于，我回家了。我花了5个月的时间欣赏美景、气候和身边知足的人。我吃健康的食品，听几乎被我忘记了的语言，在不属于我的农场里漫步，参加酿酒庆祝活动，涂上高防晒系数的防晒油抵挡阳光，连续好几天为高温烦恼。但是，还不是时候，我不能融入这样的生活，因为那个城市——伦敦，仍然留在我心里，我和她之间的爱恨情仇仍然在继续。无论开心还是不开心，我依然注定是要留在那里的。我也解释不清楚。我想这是我而不是城市的问题——我要知足。我离开了，我离开我所深爱的地方，没有什么顿悟，只不过那还不是时候。有一天家会向我走来，或者我会回家，我会心平气和地等待这一天。

My Father: Leslie Stephen

我的父亲莱斯利·斯蒂芬

Virginia Woolf

弗吉尼亚·伍尔芙

By the time that his children were growing up, the great days of my father's life were over. His feats on the river and on the mountains had been won before they were born. Relics of them were to be found lying about the house the silver cup on the study mantelpiece; the rusty alpenstocks that leaned against the bookcase in the corner; and to the end of his days he would speak of great climbers and explorers with a peculiar mixture of admiration and envy. But his own years of activity were over, and my father had to content himself with pottering about the Swiss valleys or taking a stroll across the Cornish moors.

等孩子们长大时，父亲的黄金时代已经过去了。他在高山大河大显身手时，孩子们还没有出世。但是你在屋子里到处可以发现纪念品——书房的壁炉架上有只银奖杯，屋角几支生锈的铁头登山杖靠在书橱前。到晚年他谈到出色的登山运动员和探险家时，语气之间既钦佩又忌妒，叫人难以捉摸。不过他自己生龙活虎的年月早已结束，只好在瑞士的山谷里闲逛，或者在康瓦尔郡的荒野里溜达溜达，也就满足了。

That to potter and to stroll meant more on his lips than on other people's is becoming obvious now that some of his friends have given their own version of those expeditions. He would start off after breakfast alone, or with one companion. Shortly after dinner he would return. If the walk had been successful, he would have out his great map and commemorate a new short cut in red ink. And he was quite capable, it appears, of striding all day across the moors without speaking more than a word or two to his companion. By that time, too, he had written the History of English Thought in the Eighteenth Century, which is said by some to be his masterpiece; and the Science of Ethics — the book which interested him most; and The Playground of Europe, in which is to be found "The Sunset on Mont Blanc" — in his opinion the best thing he ever wrote. He still wrote daily and methodically, though never for long at a time.

有一点越来越清楚：这些散步，听父亲说来是多么有意思，但他的朋友的说法多少有点不同。他通常在早餐后出发，有时独自一人，有时有一个游伴，晚餐以后不久他就回来了。倘若此行顺利，他会取出大幅地图，用红墨水笔标出一条新发现的捷径，以作纪念。看来有可能他在荒原各处走了一整天，跟游伴只讲过一两句话。那时他已写完了《十八世纪英国思想史》，有人认为这是他的杰作；还有《伦理学》，他自己对这本书最感兴趣；还有《欧洲游乐场》，《勃朗峰日落》一篇即收在此书中，那是他自认为写得最好的一篇文章。他每天仍旧有条不紊地写作，不过一次写不了多久。

In London he wrote in the large room with three long windows at the top of the house. He wrote lying almost recumbent in a low rocking chair which he tipped to and fro as he wrote, like a cradle, and as he wrote he smoked a short clay pipe, and he scattered books round him in a circle. The thud of a book dropped on the floor could be heard in the room beneath. And often as he mounted the stairs to his study with his firm, regular tread he would burst, not into song for he was entirely unmusical, but into a strange rhythmical chant, for verse of all kinds, both "utter trash," as he called it, and the most sublime words of Milton and Wordsworth, stuck in his memory, and the act of walking or climbing seemed to inspire him to recite whichever it was that came uppermost or suited his mood.

在伦敦时，他在一间大房间里写作，屋子一端是三排长窗。他几乎是仰靠在一张矮矮的摇椅里，一边写，一边让椅子前后摇晃，像个摇篮；同时用一支短短的陶土制的烟斗吸烟，又把书在身边撒成一圈，楼下房间里的人能听到书掉在地板上的“砰砰”声。每当他登楼到他的书房去时，他一边踏着匀称稳定的步子，一边哼哼唧唧地唱，节奏很奇特。他不是在唱歌（因为他对音乐根本不感兴趣），而是在吟诗——各种各样的诗。虽说他把诗和歌都称作“十足的废料”，却记得不少诗篇，包括弥尔顿和华兹华斯最卓越的诗句，走路或登楼，几乎一迈步就引起吟哦的兴致，什么诗句先滑到唇边，什么诗句适合他的心情，他就吟哦什么。

But it was his dexterity with his fingers that delighted his children before they could potter along the lanes at his heels or read his books. He would twist a sheet of paper beneath a pair of scissors and out would drop an elephant, a stag, or a monkey, with trunks, horns, and tails delicately and exactly formed. Or, taking a pencil, he would draw beast after beast — an art that he practiced almost unconsciously as he read, so that the flyleaves of his books swarm with owls and donkeys as if to illustrate the "Oh, you ass!" or "Conceited dunce" that he was wont to scribble impatiently in the margin. Such brief comments, in which one may find the germ of the more temperate statements of his essays, recall some of the characteristics of his talk. He could be very silent, as his friends have testified. But his remarks, made suddenly in a low voice between the puffs of his pipe, were extremely effective. Sometimes with one word — but his one word was accompanied by a gesture of the hand — he would dispose of the tissue of exaggerations which his own sobriety seemed to provoke. "There are 40,000,000 unmarried women in London alone!" Lady Ritchie once informed him. "Oh, Annie, Annie!" my father exclaimed in tones of horrified but affectionate rebuke. But Lady Ritchie, as if she enjoyed being rebuked, would pile it up even higher next time she came.

可是，当他的孩子们还小，还不能跟着他在小巷里闲逛，也不会读他写的书，给孩子们带来乐趣的是他灵巧的手指。他会将一张纸折几折，拿剪刀一剪，就剪出一头象，一头公鹿，或者一只猴子，有长鼻子，有角，有尾巴，样子像极了。要不然就拿起一支铅笔画野兽，画了一只又一只。这画画的本领是随着他看书不知不觉地练出来的。他看书时惯于在页边空白处不耐烦地信手写上“啊，你这蠢驴!”或是“自以为了不起的笨蛋”，书的衬页上就画满了猫头鹰和驴子，仿佛是为那些评语做插图。你可以发现，在他自己写的文章里，这类尖锐的评语却化为温和的意见。这种情况可以使人回忆起他跟人交谈时的某些特征。正如他的朋友所证明的那样，他能好些时候一言不发，只管自吸烟斗。可是，等他突然停止吸烟，小声儿提出他的看法，意见却十分中肯。有时候似乎是他自己的过分冷静引起对方连篇的夸张，他会用片言只语把对方的话打发掉——这片言只语总伴随着一定的手势。有一次里奇夫人告诉他：“单伦敦一地，就有4000万未婚妇女!”“啊，安妮，安妮!”父亲大声说，那音调表示不胜惊骇，又带着深情的责备。可是里奇夫人似乎以受责备为乐，下一次来访时还会加码。

The stories he told to amuse his children of adventures in the Alps — but accidents only happened, he would explain, if you were so foolish as to disobey your guides — or of those long walks, after one of which, from Cambridge to London on a lot day, "I drank, I am sorry to say, rather more than was good for me," were told very briefly, but with a curious power to impress the scene. The things that he did not say were always there in the background. So, too, though he seldom told anecdotes, and his memory for facts was bad, when he described a person — and he had known many people, both famous and obscure — he would convey exactly what he thought of him in two or three words. And what he thought might be the opposite of what other people thought. He had a way of upsetting established reputations and disregarding conventional values that could be disconcerting and sometimes perhaps wounding, though no one was more respectful of any feeling that seemed to him genuine. But when, suddenly opening his bright blue eyes and rousing himself from what had seemed complete abstraction, he gave his opinion, it was difficult to disregard it. It was a habit, especially when deafness made him unaware that this opinion could be heard, that had its inconveniences.

"I am the most easily bored of men," he wrote, truthfully as usual; and when, as was inevitable in a large family, some visitor threatened to stay not merely for tea but also for dinner, my father would express his anguish at first by twisting and untwisting a certain lock of hair. Then he would burst out, half to himself, half to the powers above, but quite audibly, "Why can't he go? Why can't he go?" Yet such is the charm of simplicity — and did he not say, also truthfully, that "bores are the salt of the earth"? — that the bores seldom went, or, if they did, forgave him and came again.

他给孩子们讲故事玩，讲在阿尔卑斯山脉的探险故事时他会解释，除非你愚蠢得不听向导的话，不会发生什么意外的；讲到历次长途步行，有一次在一个大热天从剑桥走到伦敦，到达后“我拼命喝水，说来好笑，喝得过了头。”这些故事他说得虽简单，能引人入胜，使人如临其境。他没有讲出来的东西你总可以自己想象得出。谈论人物的时候也是如此，虽说他难得讲故事，记性也不好。他认得许多人，有的是著名人物，有的是无名之辈，当他描述一个人的时候，三言两语，就准确地说出他对此人的看法，而他的看法可能同别人的看法恰恰相反。他惯于推翻公认的声望，无视传统的价值观，因而使别人感到为难，有时也不免伤了别人的感情，不过凡是他认为真诚的感情，没有人能像他这样尊重。而当他突然睁开明亮的蓝眼睛，仿佛是从十分出神的状态中苏醒过来，发表他的意见时，谁要是不重视这意见是很难办到的。这种习惯也有其不便之处，特别是后来他的耳朵聋了，不知道别人能不能听到他的意见。

“我这个人最容易感到厌烦，”他以一贯的真诚写道。一个大家庭里难免有这样的情形：有时来了客人，看来吃过午后的茶点还不想告辞，还要等着吃晚饭，父亲不耐烦了，先是揪住一绺头发，捻过来又捻过去，以表示他的苦恼；后来就发作了，半对自己，半对过往神灵，但是话音完全可以听得清：“他为什么不肯走？他为什么不肯走？”不过直率的性格就是如此迷人。——再说，他不是同样真诚地说过“惹人厌烦的人是高尚的人”？——他还说过，惹人厌的人很少肯走；要是走了，就请原谅他，改天再来吧。

Too much, perhaps, has been said of his silence; too much stress has been laid upon his reserve. He loved clear thinking; he hated sentimentality and gush; but this by no means meant that he was cold and unemotional, perpetually critical and condemnatory in daily life. On the contrary, it was his power of feeling strongly and of expressing his feeling with vigor that made him sometimes so alarming as a companion. A lady, for instance, complained of the wet summer that was spoiling her tour in Cornwall. But to my father, though he never called himself a democrat, the rain meant that the corn was being laid; some poor man was being ruined; and the energy with which he expressed his sympathy — not with the lady — left her discomfited. He had something of the same respect for farmers and fishermen that he had for climbers and explorers. So, too, he talked little of patriotism, but during the South African War — and all wars were hateful to him — he lay awake thinking that he heard the guns on the battlefield. Again, neither his reason nor his cold common sense helped to convince him that a child could be late for dinner without having been maimed or killed in an accident. And not all his mathematics together with a bank balance which he insisted must be ample in the extreme could persuade him, when it came to signing a check, that the whole family was not "shooting Niagara to ruin," as he put it. The pictures that he would draw of old age and the bankruptcy court, of ruined men of letters who have to support large families in small houses at Wimbledon (he owned a very small house at Wimbledon), might have convinced those who complain of his understatements that hyperbole was well within his reach had he chosen.

Yet the unreasonable mood was superficial, as the rapidity with which it vanished would prove. The checkbook was shut; Wimbledon and the workhouse were forgotten. Some thought of a humorous kind made him chuckle. Taking his hat and his stick, calling for his dog and his daughter, he would stride off into

Kensington Gardens, where he had walked as a little boy, where his brother Fitzjames and he had made beautiful bows to young Queen Victoria and she had swept them a curtsy; and so, round the Serpentine to Hyde Park Corner, where he had once saluted the great Duke himself; and so home. He was not then in the least "alarming"; he was very simple, very confiding; and his silence, though one might last unbroken from the Round Pond to the Marble Arch, was curiously full of meaning, as if he were thinking, half aloud, about poetry and philosophy and people he had known.

He himself was the most abstemious of men. He smoked a pipe perpetually, but never a cigar. He wore his clothes until they were too shabby to be tolerable; and he held old-fashioned and rather puritanical views as to the vice of luxury and the sin of idleness. The relations between parents and children today have a freedom that would have been impossible with my father. He expected a certain standard of behavior, even of ceremony, in family life. Yet if freedom means the right to think one's own thoughts and to follow one's own pursuits, then no one respected and indeed insisted upon freedom more completely than he did. His sons, with the exception of the Army and Navy, should follow whatever professions they chose; his daughters, though he cared little enough for the higher education of women, should have the same liberty. If at one moment he rebuked a daughter sharply for smoking a cigarette — smoking was not in his opinion a nice habit in the other sex — she had only to ask him if she might become a painter, and he assured her that so long as she took her work seriously he would give her all the help he could. He had no special love for painting; but he kept his word. Freedom of that sort was worth thousands of cigarettes.

或许人们过多地谈到他的沉默，过分地强调他的冷淡。确实，他喜欢冷静地思考，厌恶感情冲动，但这并不意味着他是冷冰冰地毫无感情，也不是对日常生活动辄批评和谴责。恰恰相反，他有时候感情强烈，而且能有力地表达他的感情，甚至使别人感到吃惊。譬如，一位太太埋怨夏

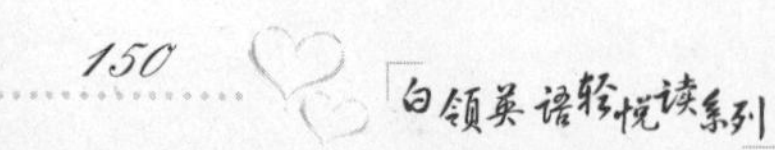

天雨水过多，使她的康瓦尔郡之游败了兴。我父亲虽说从来不曾自命为民主主义者，可是对他来说，大雨意味着庄稼倒伏，有些穷人要遭殃。他的同情——不是对那位太太的——表达得极其有力，使她感到狼狈。他对农民和渔民颇为敬重，就像他对登山运动员和探险家一样。同样，他也很少谈到爱国主义。可是，尽管他憎恨一切战争，而在南非战争期间，他躺在床上睡不着，觉得自己听到战场上的枪炮声。另一方面，即使凭他的理智和冷静的常识，他也不肯相信，倘若一个孩子到吃晚饭时还没有回来，就一定是遭到事故，非死即伤。而每当他签一张支票的时候，他的全部数学头脑加上银行存款——他坚信银行存款必须极其富裕——也无法使他相信他全家不致遭灭顶之灾——如他所说，等于驾条小船去尼亚加拉大瀑布。他惯常给家里人描绘这样的图画：老年人在法庭上宣告破产；潦倒的文人要养活一大家子，挤在温伯顿的小屋子里（父亲在温伯顿有一所很小的房子）。这足以使那些埋怨他说话爱含蓄的人相信，倘若他愿意的话，要夸张也是毫不费事的。

不过这种超乎常情的状态只是表面，从它很快消失就可以证明。支票簿合上了，温伯顿和济贫院也丢到脑后了。他想到什么幽默的事，不禁吃吃地笑，于是拿起帽子和手杖，招呼一声狗和女儿，迈步走向肯辛顿王家公园。他从小就在这公园里散步，就在这里他和他的哥哥菲茨詹姆士曾向年轻的维多利亚女王漂亮地鞠躬，而女王也很快地还礼；同样，在塞平太恩到海德公园角附近，他曾经向威灵顿公爵本人致敬。走过这些地方，他就回家了。这时候他一点也不叫人“吃惊”，他非常单纯，对人完全信任；尽管从圆塘到大理石拱门，他没有说过一句话，他这种沉默却充满不寻常的意义，仿佛在内心自言自语，谈到诗歌、哲学以及他认得的人。

他自己是个最节俭的人。他始终只吸烟斗，从不吸雪茄。他的衣服要穿到褴褛不堪；对于奢侈和懒惰这两种罪恶，他保持着旧式的甚至是清教徒式的观点。当今父母和子女之间的关系比较自由，但对我父亲来说恐怕行不通。他希望在家庭生活中保持一定的行为准则，甚至礼节。不过，如果自由指的是独立思考的权利、追求自己理想的权利，那么，没有任何人像父亲那样绝对尊重并坚决维护这种自由。他的儿子们可以从事自己选定的任何职业，除了陆军和海军，虽说他不大关心女子受高等教育，但他的女儿也有同样的自由。如果说他刚才还为女儿抽了一支烟而痛骂了她一顿（她认为女子抽烟不是个好习惯），她只消问起他可不可以当画家，他就会郑重表示：只要她认真从事这项工作，他会给予力所能及的任何帮助。他对绘画并没有特别爱好，但他决不食言。这一种自由值成千上万支香烟。

It was the same with the perhaps more difficult problem of literature. Even today there may be parents who would doubt the wisdom of allowing a girl of fifteen the free run of a large and quite unexpurgated library. But my father allowed it. There were certain facts — very briefly, very shyly he referred to them. Yet "Read what you like," he said, and all his books, "mangy and worthless," as he called them, but certainly they were many and various, were to be had without asking. To read what one liked because one liked it, never to pretend to admire what one did not — that was his only lesson in the art of reading. To write in the fewest possible words, as clearly as possible, exactly what one meant — that was his only lesson in the art of writing. All the rest must be learned for oneself. Yet a child must have been childish in the extreme not to feel that such was the teaching of a man great learning and wide experience, though he would never impose his own views or parade his own knowledge. For, as his tailor remarked when he saw my father walk past his shop up Bond Street, "There goes a gentleman that wears good clothes without knowing it."

In those last years, grown solitary and very deaf, he would sometimes call himself a failure as a writer, grown solitary and very deaf, he would sometimes call himself whether he failed or succeeded as a writer, it is permissible to believe that he left a distinct impression of himself on the minds of his friends. Meredith saw him as "Phoebus Apollo turned fasting friar" in his earlier days; Thomas Hardy, years later, looked at the "spare and desolate figure" of the Schreckhorn and thought of him,

Who scaled its horn with ventured life and limb,
Drawn on by vague imaginings, maybe,
Of semblance to his personality
In its quaint glooms, keen lights, and rugged trim.

对于文学作品这个或许是更困难的问题，他的态度也是一样。即使在今天，有些做父母的也不免怀疑，让15岁的女孩自由阅读大量未经删节的图书是否明智，而我的父亲容许这样做。确实有些不堪入目的东西——他非常简短、隐隐约约地谈起这些东西。可是他还是说，“你爱读什么就读什么”，而他的全部藏书，尽管照他说是“滥而无用”，数量却不少，范围也很广，我们用不着征求他的意见就可以拿来看。因为你爱它，你就读它；你不喜欢书，决不要装作喜欢它——这就是他对读书艺术的唯一教导。他对写作技巧的唯一教导是：词句要简洁、清楚，表达要十分准确。其余的，全靠自己摸索。可是孩子总是极端幼稚，不能体会到这就是一个有学问、有丰富经验的人的教导，虽说他从不会把自己的观点强加于人，也不会炫耀自己的学识。诚如他的裁缝师傅有一次看见他在邦德街走过他的铺子门口时说：“刚才走过去的那位先生，穿着漂亮衣服，自己却不知道好在哪里。”

在他一生的最后几年间，他变得更孤寂，聋得更厉害，有时称自己是个失败的作家，半瓶醋。姑且不论他是成功的作家还是失败的作家，可以相信他给朋友们留下了深刻的印象。梅瑞狄斯把年青时代的他比作“太阳神阿波罗变成苦行僧”；汤姆斯·哈代若干年后眺望着希瑞克杭峰“瘦削而孤寂的形象”时想到他，

无谓的生命和躯体向峰顶攀登，
模糊的想象吸引着他不断前进，
那山峰或许跟他的人品相似：
奇异的幽暗，耀眼的光芒和崎岖的外形。

But the praise he would have valued most, for though he was an agnostic nobody believed more profoundly in the worth of human relationships, was Meredith's tribute after his death: "He was the one man to my knowledge worthy to have married your mother." And Lowell, when he called him "L. S., the most lovable of men," has best described the quality that makes him, after all these years, unforgettable.

不过，最可能引起父亲重视的，是他死后梅瑞狄斯的赞语："就我所知，只有他才配得上你的母亲"，因为，虽然父亲是一个不可知论者，他却比任何人都更深信亲属关系的价值。而洛厄尔则称他为"最可爱的人"，最出色地描绘了他的品质，使他在逝世这么些年以后仍令人难忘。

Love Your Mother than You Love Yourself

爱你的妈妈要甚于爱你自己

Anonymous/佚名

◆ **Those Childhood Days**

童年时光

When you came into the world, she held you in her arms.

你来到人世，她抱你在怀。

You thanked her by weeping your eyes out.

你报答她，哭得天昏地暗。

When you were 1 year old, she fed you and bathed you.

你1岁时，她为你哺乳，为你洗澡。

You thanked her by crying all night long.

你报答她，哭了个通宵。

When you were 2 years old, she taught you to walk.

你2岁时，她教你走路。

You thanked her by running away when she called.

你报答她，她一叫你就跑。

When you were 3 years old, she made all your meals with love.

你3岁时，她满怀爱心为你准备三餐。

You thanked her by tossing your plate on the floor.

你报答她，把盘子一抛摔在地。

When you were 4 years old, she gave you some crayons.

你4岁时，她给你几支彩笔。

You thanked her by coloring the dining room table.

你报答她，把餐桌涂成大花脸。

When you were 5 years old, she dressed you for the holidays.

你5岁时，节日里他盛装打扮你。

You thanked her by plopping into the nearest pile of mud.

你报答她，扑通一声摔进旁边一堆泥巴里。

When you were 6 years old, she walked you to school.

你6岁时，她步行送你去上学。

You thanked her by screaming "I'm not going!"

你报答她，扯着嗓子叫："我就是不去!"

When you were 7 years old, she bought you a baseball.

你7岁时，她给你买来个棒球。

You thanked her by throwing it through the next-door-neighbor's window.

你报答她，把邻居玻璃砸得稀里哗啦。

When you were 8 years old, she handed you an ice cream.

你8岁时，她递给你一支冰淇淋。

You thanked her by dripping it all over your lap.

你报答她，都是些滴在你膝盖上的冰淇淋水。

When you were 9 years old, she paid for piano lessons.

你9岁时，她掏钱让你学钢琴。

You thanked her by never even bothering to practice.

你报答她，从来不用心去练它。

When you were 10 years old, she drove you all day, from soccer to gymnastics to one birthday party after another.

你10岁时，她整天开车为你忙，从足球场到健身房，到一个又一个的生日会场。

You thanked her by jumping out of the car and never looking back.

你报答她，跳下车，头也不回地背朝她。

When you were 11 years old, she took you and your friends to the movies.

你11岁，她带你和朋友去影院。

You thanked her by asking to sit in a different row.

你报答她，请她坐到另一排。

When you were 12 years old, she warned you not to watch certain TV shows.

你12岁，她警告你有些电视不要看。

You thanked her by waiting until she left the house.

你报答她，等她离开偏要看。

◆ **Those Teenage Years**

少年岁月

When you were 13, she suggested a haircut that was becoming.

你13岁，她建议你把发型剪得体。

You thanked her by telling her she had no taste.

你报答她，对她连说没品位。

When you were 14, she paid for a month away at summer camp.

你14岁，她掏钱送你进夏令营。

You thanked her by forgetting to write a single letter.

你报答她，整月没有一封信。

When you were 15, she came home from work, looking for a hug.

15岁时，她下班回到家，希望有人拥抱她。

You thanked her by having your bedroom door locked.

你报答她，把房门反锁不理她。

When your were 16, she taught you how to drive her car.

你16岁时，她手把手教你开她的车。

You thanked her by taking it every chance you could.

你报答她，逮着机会就玩车。

When you were 17, she was expecting an important call.

你17岁时，她在等一个重要电话，

You thanked her by being on the phone all night.

你报答她，电话被你占线了一通宵。

When you were 18, she cried at your high school graduation.

18岁你高中毕业时，她喜极而泣把泪洒。

You thanked her by staying out partying until dawn.

你报答她，在外面聚会通宵达旦不回家。

◆ Growing Old and Gray

成人、渐老

When you were 19, she paid your college tuition, drove you to campus, carried your bags.

你19岁，大学学费她买单，扛着包开车送你到学校。

You thanked her by saying good-bye outside the dorm so you wouldn't be embarrassed in front of your friends.

你报答她，在宿舍门外说再见，为的是不在朋友面前现大眼。

When you were 20, she asked whether you were seeing anyone.

你20岁时，她问你是否在约会。

You thanked her by saying, "It's none of your business."

你报答她，对她说："这事不管不行吗。"

When you were 21, she suggested certain careers for your future.

你21岁，她为你将来事业提建议。

You thanked her by saying, "I don't want to be like you."

你报答她，对她说，"我才不愿学你那样呢。"

When you were 22, she hugged you at your college graduation.

你22岁，大学毕业典礼上，她伸手把你紧拥抱。

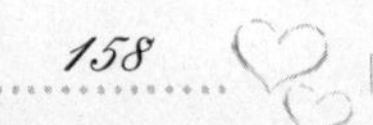

You thanked her by asking whether she could pay for a trip to Europe.

你报答她，问她能否掏钱让你到欧洲逛一趟。

When you were 23, she gave you furniture for your first apartment.

你23岁，她为你第一套公寓置家具。

You thanked her by telling your friends it was ugly.

你报答她，告诉朋友家具的模样丑。

When you were 24, she met your fiancé and asked about your plans for the future.

你24岁，她遇到你的未婚夫，问你们将来有何打算。

You thanked her by glaring and growing, "Muuhh-ther, please!"

你报答她，对她怒目加咆哮，"妈……，得了吧，求你啦！"

When you were 25, she helped to pay for your wedding, and she cried and told you how deeply she loved you.

你25岁，她花钱帮你筹办婚礼，哭诉深深爱着你。

You thanked her by moving halfway across the country.

你报答她，安家离她千万里。

When you were 30, she called with some advice on the baby.

你30岁，她打来电话为宝宝抚养提忠告。

You thanked her by telling her, "Things are different now."

你报答她，告诉她："如今情况不同啦！"

When you were 40, she called to remind you of a relative's birthday.

你40岁，她打电话来提醒，亲戚的生日勿忘记。

You thanked her by saying you were "really busy right now".

你报答她，说你"实在太忙。"

When you were 50, she fell ill and needed you to take care of her.

你50岁，她病倒需要你照顾。

You thanked her by reading about the burden parents become to their children.

你报答她，念叨父母成负担。

And then one day she quietly died.

后来有一天，她悄悄地去了。

And everything you never did came crashing down like thunder.

突然间，你该做未做的事，仿佛霹雳，在你耳边炸响。

"Rock me baby, rock me all night long."

"摇啊摇，摇我这个小宝宝，一夜到天亮。"

"The hand who rocks the cradle... may rock the world."

"摇摇篮的手啊……可以摇世界。"

Let us take a moment of the time just to pay tribute and show appreciation to the person called mom though some may not say it openly to their mother. There's no substitute for her. Cherish every single moment. Though at times she may not be the best of friends, may not agree to our thoughts, she is still your mother! She will be there for you... to listen to your woes, your braggings, your frustations, etc. Ask yourself... have you put aside enough time for her, to listen to her "blues" of working in the kitchen, her tiredness? Be tactful, loving and still show her due respect though you may have a different view from hers. Once gone, only fond memories of the past and also regrets will be left.

让我们花一小会儿时间，对那个叫"妈"的人表示敬意，表达感谢，虽然有些人当着面说不出口。妈妈是不可替代的。珍惜与她在一起的每一时刻吧。虽然有时候，她可能不是我们最好的朋友，可能不同意我们的想法，但妈妈就是妈妈！她始终陪伴你身边，听你的伤心事，听你吹大牛，听你把沮丧倾诉……扪心自问，你是否曾经抽出过足够的时间陪伴她，听她讲围着灶台转的"伤心事"，讲她也会疲劳？就算你与她意见不一，也要委婉，充满爱心，对她表示出应有的尊敬。一旦她去了，剩下的就只有对过去岁月的美好回忆，还有就是终生的遗憾。

Don't take for granted the things closest to your heart. Love her more than you love yourself. Life is meaningless without her...

不要以为，与你心最近，你就理所应得。爱她，要甚于爱自己。生命中没有了她，将了无意义……

A Good Heart to Lean on

善心可依

Anonymous/佚名

When I was growing up, I was embarrassed to be seen with my father. He was severely crippled and very short, and when we would walk together, his hand on my arm for balance, people would stare. I would inwardly squirm at the unwanted attention. If he ever noticed or was bothered, he never let on. It was difficult to coordinate our steps — his halting, mine impatient — and because of that, we didn't say much as we went along. But as we started out, he always said, "You set the pace. I will try to adjust to you."

Our usual walk was to or from the subway, which was how he got to work. He went to work sick, and despite nasty weather. He almost never missed a day, and would make it to the office even if others could not. A matter of pride.

When snow or ice was on the ground, it was impossible for him to walk, even with help. At such times my sisters or I would pull him through the streets of Brooklyn, NY, on a child's sleigh to the subway entrance. Once there, he would cling to the handrail until he reached the lower steps that the warmer tunnel air kept ice-free. In Manhattan the subway station was the basement of his office building, and he would not have to go outside again until we met him in Brooklyn' on his way home.

When I think of it now, I marvel at how much courage it must have taken for a grown man to subject himself to such indignity and stress. And at how he did it — without bitterness or complaint.

He never talked about himself as an object of pity, nor did he show any envy of the more fortunate or able. What he looked for in others was a "good heart", and if he found one, the owner was good enough for him.

Now that I am older, I believe that is a proper standard by which to judge people, even though I still don' t know precisely what a "good heart" is. But I know the times I don't have one myself.

Unable to engage in many activities, my father still tried to participate in some way. When a local sandlot baseball team found itself without a manager, he kept it going. He was a knowledgeable baseball fan and often took me to Ebbets Field to see the Brooklyn Dodgers play. He liked to go to dances and parties, where he could have a good time just sitting and watching.

On one memorable occasion a fight broke out at a beach party, with everyone punching and shoving. He wasn't content to sit and watch, but he couldn't stand unaided on the soft sand. In frustration he began to shout, "I' ll fight anyone who will tit down with me!"

Nobody did. But the next day people kidded him by saying it was the first time any fighter was urged to take a dive even before the bout began.

I now know he participated in some things vicariously through me, his only son. When I played ball (poorly), he "played" too. When I joined the Navy he "joined" too. And when I came home on leave, he saw to it that I visited his office. Introducing me, he was really saying, "This is my son, but it is also me, and I could have done this, too, if things had been different." Those words were never said aloud.

He has been gone many years now, but I think of him often. I wonder if he sensed my reluctance to be seen with him during our walks. If he did, I am sorry I never told him how sorry I was, how unworthy I was, how I regretted it. I think of him when I complain about trifles, when I am envious of another's good fortune, when I don't have a "good heart". At such times I put my hand on his arm to regain my balance, and say, "You set the pace, I will try to adjust to you."

在我成长的过程中，我一直羞于让别人看见和父亲在一起。我的父亲身材矮小，腿上有严重的残疾。当我们一起走路时，他总是挽着我以保持身体平衡，这时总招来一些异样的目光，令我无地自容。可是如果他注意到了这些，不管他内心多么痛苦，也从不表现出来。

走路时，我们很难相互协调起来——他的步子慢慢腾腾，我的步子焦躁不安。所以一路上我们交谈得很少。但是每次出行前，他总是说，“你走你的，我想法儿跟上你”。

我们常常往返于从家到他上班乘坐的地铁站的那段路上。他有病也要上班，哪怕天气恶劣。他几乎从未误过一天工，就是在别人不能去的情况下，他也要设法去上班。实在值得骄傲！

每当冰封大地，雪花飘飘的时候，若是没有帮助，他简直举步维艰。每当此时，我或我的姐妹们就用儿童雪橇把他拉过纽约布鲁克林区的街道，一直送他到地铁的入口处。一到那儿，他便手抓扶手一直走到底下的台阶时才放开手，因为那里通道的空气暖和些，地面上没有结冰。到了曼哈顿，地铁站就在他办公楼的地下一层，在我们从布鲁克林接他回家之前他无须再走出楼来。

如今每当我想起这些，我惊叹一个成年男子要经受住这种侮辱和压力得需要多么大的勇气啊！叹服他竟然能够做到这一点，不带任何痛苦，没有丝毫抱怨。

他从不说自己可怜，也从不嫉妒别人的幸运和能力。他所期望的是人家“善良的心”，当他发现时，拥有者真的对他很好。

如今我已经长大成人，我明白了“善良的心”是评价人的恰当的标准，尽管我仍不很清楚它的确切涵义，但是我却知道我有缺乏善心的时候。

虽然父亲不能参加许多活动，但他仍然设法以某种方式参与进来。当一个地方棒球队发现缺少一个领队时，他便作了领队。因为他是个棒球迷，有丰富的棒球知识，他过去常带我去埃比茨棒球场观看布鲁克林的鬼精灵队的比赛。他喜欢参加舞会和晚会，乐意坐着看。

记得有一次的海边晚会上，有人打架，动了拳头，推推搡搡。他不甘于坐在那里当观众，但又无法在松软的沙滩上自己站起来。于是，失望之下，他吼了起来：“谁想坐下和我打？”

没有人响应。但是第二天，人们都取笑他说比赛还没开始，拳击手就被劝认输，这还是头一次看见。

现在我知道一些事情他是通过我——他唯一的儿子来做的。当我打球时（尽管我打得很差），他也在“打球”。当我参加海军时，他也“参加”。当时我回家休息时，他一定要让我去他的办公室，在介绍我时，他真真切切地说，“这是我儿子，但也是我自己，假如事情不是这样的话，我也会这样做的。”那些话从未大声说过。

父亲离开我们已经很多年了，但是我时常想起他。我不知道他是否意识到我曾经不愿意让人看到和他走在一起的心理。假如他知道这一切，我现在感到很遗憾，因为我从没告诉过他我是多么愧疚、多么不孝、多么悔恨。每当我为一些琐事抱怨时，为别人的好运而妒忌时，为我自己缺乏“善心”时，我就会想起我的父亲。此时，我会挽着他的胳膊保持身体平衡，并且说，“你走你的，我想法儿跟上你。”

Dance with My Father

和爸爸跳舞

Anonymous/佚名

Back when I was a child, before life removed all the innocence,
My father would lift me high and dance with my mother and me and then
Spin me around till I fell asleep.
Then up the stairs he would carry me
And I knew for sure I was loved.
If I could get another chance, another walk, another dance with him,
I'd play a song that would never, ever end.
How I'd love, love, love
To dance with my father again.
When I and my mother would disagree

小时候，生活还没有带走所有的天真，
爸爸常常把我高高举起，跟妈妈和我跳舞，然后
抱着我旋转直到我睡着。
然后他抱我上楼，
我敢肯定，他爱着我。
如果再有一次机会，和他一起走路，和他一起跳舞，
我一定要唱一首永远永远不休止的歌。
我会多么多么多么欢喜
能和爸爸再跳一次舞。
每当妈妈不听我的话，

To get my way, I would run from her to him.

He'd make me laugh just to comfort me,

Then finally make me do just what my mama said.

Later that night when I was asleep,

He left a dollar under my sheet,

Never dreamed that he would be gone from me.

If I could steal one final glance, one final step, one final dance with him,

I'd play a song that would never, ever end,

Cause I'd love, love, love

To dance with my father again.

Sometimes I'd listen outside her door,

And I'd hear how my mother cried for him.

I pray for her even more than me.

我就从她那里跑开去找爸爸。

他总能让我笑起来，给我安慰，

然后乖乖地照妈妈说的去做。

那一天深夜，我睡得很香，

他在我的床单下塞了一块钱，

我做梦也没想到他会从此离开我。

假如我能看他最后一眼，他最后的脚步，和他跳最后一次舞，

我一定要唱一首永远永远不休止的歌，因为我多么多么多么欢喜

能和爸爸再跳一次舞。

有时我会在妈妈的房门外偷听，

我知道她为他哭得有多伤心。

我为自己祈祷，更为她祈祷。

I know I'm praying for much too much,

But could you send back the only man she loved.

I know you don't do it usually

But dear Lord, she's dying.

To dance with my father again,

Every night I fall asleep and this is all I ever dream.

我知道我祈求得实在太多，

但你能不能把她爱的唯一的男人送回。

我知道你一般不这么做

可是亲爱的上帝啊，她快要死了。

为了和爸爸再跳一次舞，

每天晚上我都睡着，而这就是我全部的梦。

Feeling Father's Love

感受父爱

Anonymous/佚名

Daddy just didn't know how to show love. It was Mom who held the family together. He just went to work every day and came home and she'd have a list of sins we'd committed and he would scold us about them.

Once when I stole a candy bar, he made me take it back and tell the man I stole it and that I'd unpack boxes to pay for it. But it was Mom who understood I was just a kid.

I broke my leg once on the playground swing and it was Mom who held me in her arms all the way to the hospital. Dad pulled the car right up to the door of the emergency room and when they asked him to move it because that space was reserved for emergency vehicles. He shouted, "What do you think this is? A tour bus?"

爸爸根本不知道如何表达爱，把这个家维系在一起的人是妈妈。爸爸只是天天去上班，回家后，妈妈向他数落我们所做的一连串错事，于是爸爸在为了这些事把我们责骂一通。

有一次我偷了一个棒棒糖。爸爸硬要我送回去，让我告诉卖糖的人那是我偷的，并说我愿意帮他拆箱开包作为赔偿。但妈妈却理解我，她知道我只不过是个孩子。

还有一次我在操场荡秋千摔坏了腿，一路抱着我到医院的人是妈妈。爸爸将车正好停在急诊室门口。因为那儿是专供急救车停靠的，医院里的人就叫爸爸把车开走。爸爸大吼起来："你以为这是什么车？难道是旅游车吗？"

At my birthday parties, Dad always seemed sort of out of place. He just busied himself blowing up balloons, and setting up tables, and running errands. It was Mom how carried in the cake with candles on it for me to blow out.

When I leaf through picture albums, people always ask, "What does your Dad look like?" Who knows? He was always fiddling around with the camera taking everyone else's picture. I must have a zillion pictures of Mom and me smiling together.

I remember when Mom told him to teach me how to ride a bicycle. I told him not to let go, but he said it was time. I fell and Mom ran to pick me up, but he waved her off. I was so mad, but I showed him. I got right back on that bike and rode it myself. He didn't even feel embarrassed, he just smiled.

在我的生日聚会上，爸爸总显得有点如坐针毡。他不是忙于吹气球，就是摆桌子，或做些跑腿的活儿。将插满蜡烛的生日蛋糕捧进来让我吹灭的人总是妈妈。

我随便翻阅相册时，别人总会问：“你爸爸长什么模样？”还真说不出。他总是摆弄着相机为别人拍照。我和妈妈在一起微笑的照片一定多得都数不清了。

还记得有一次妈妈叫爸爸教我骑自行车。我叫他扶着车子别松手，他却说是松手的时候了。我摔了下来，妈妈跑来扶我，他却挥手示意让妈妈走开。我真是气得发疯，决心非要让他看看我的本事不可。我马上骑上车，竟能一个人骑了。爸爸却一点也不尴尬，只是笑笑。

When I went to college, Mom did all the writing. He just sent checks and a little note about how great his lawn looked in that I wasn't playing football on it.

Whenever I called home, he acted like he wanted to talk, but he always said, "I'll get your mother."

When I got married, it was Mom who cried. He just blew his nose loudly and left the room.

All my life he said, "Where are you going? What time are you coming home? No, you cannot go." Daddy just didn't know how to show love. Unless…

Is it possible he showed it and I didn't recognize it?

上大学了，给我写信的总是妈妈。爸爸只是寄来支票，还有一张小便条，说草坪因我不再上面踢足球，现在长得好极了。

每次我打电话回家，爸爸总像是有话要说，但结果他总是说："我叫你妈来接。"

我结婚的时候，妈妈哭了，爸爸只是大声地擤擤鼻子，离开了房间。

在我的一生中，他总是说："你去哪儿？什么时候回家？不行，你不能去。"爸爸完全不知道怎样表达爱。除非……

会不会是他已经表达了而我却没有意识到呢？

Great Parents
可怜天下父母心

Anonymous/佚名

It's September again. Again, I see the different facial expressions of the parents taking their children to college.

It's mostly the male parents who perform this duty. Sometimes both parents come. The highly personalized faces which usually differ from each other in a thousand and one ways fade at this moment into each other, and display the same look: fatigue, exhaustion, the timidness and cautiousness of a new comer, and the concernedness and fear that their offspring might be treated unfairly.

又到了9月。同样，我又看到了来送孩子们上大学的父母们脸上各种各样的表情。

大部分是父亲来送。有时候父母都来。这些平时截然不同的、具有高度个人色彩的脸庞在这个时刻变得一样，而且表现出同样的神情：疲劳，精疲力尽，新来者的那种胆小谨慎，还有担忧和害怕，怕自己的孩子遭到不公正的待遇。

Such long and exhausting journeys over here! So many complicated and time-consuming procedures! They corrode people's elan. The gleefulness and dizziness usually found in "eighteen-year-old youngsters who've made it" disappear altogether. Close on the heels of their parents, they shuffle from place to place in the campus. To go through one formality, they have to talk long distances and ask many questions of many people, and their parents have to smile politely all the time. Everywhere they have to line up and to pay. The sun being blazing, they find themselves perspiring all over. They have to sit by the roadside for a rest and satisfy their thirst by drinking bottled water whose prices soar because of scarcity. No matter how dignified and classy one may look on other days, one has to, for the sake of one's children, humble oneself, put up with inconveniences, and show one's best smiles to find out what to do. I saw a father carrying a huge bed-roll. Bent with the heavy burden on his shoulder, he had to strain for a look ahead in order to see the way forward. His son, head hanging low, followed behind with only a small bag. It won't be long before his boy will help the girls with their bags.

那么长，那么累的旅程！那么繁琐费时的手续！他们挫去了人们的锐气。那些意气风发的18岁少年们常有的欢乐和光环没有了，他们紧跟着父母，在校园里从一个地方赶到另一个地方。为完成一个手续，他们不得不走很远的距离，向很多人咨询各种问题，他们的父母一直保持着礼貌的微笑。到处都要排队。太阳火辣辣的，他们全身都湿透了。他们不得不在路边坐下来休息一下，喝那些由于紧缺而价格飞涨的瓶装水来解渴。无论平时他们是如何尊贵，如何有风度，现在不得不为了自己的孩子卑躬屈膝，忍受各种不便，用自己最好的微笑来打听下一步怎么做。我看见一个父亲扛着巨大的铺盖卷。由于这沉重的负担，他不得不弯着腰，却努力向前看着应该走哪条路。他的儿子，低着头跟在后面，手里只拿着一个很小的包。很快，这个男孩就会给其他女孩子们扛包了。

I also saw a father and son coming near hand in hand from the fork of a road. A mere glance told me that they are from one of the poor rural areas. Both wore cheap T-shirts and had crew-cuts. Even smaller in build, the old man has graying hair and a tan. An arrogant taxi sped towards them and was on the point of knocking down the oldster. The poor man quickly jumped aside. It was a near escape. Then, only then, was he separated from his son. When the car shot past, they joined hands again, continued on their way, each being the other's support.

The sight nearly brought tears to my eyes.

我还看见一对父子手拉着手从岔道那儿走过来。一看就知道他们来自贫苦的山区。两个人都穿着廉价的T恤衫，同样的平头。父亲的身材更矮小一些，头发已经花白，脸色黝黑。一辆趾高气昂的出租车飞快开过去，差点撞到那个父亲。这个可怜的老人迅速跳到一边。差一点就撞到了。只有那一瞬他才和儿子分开。当车开过之后，他们又牵着手，继续向前走，相互支持着对方。

这一幕让我几乎流出泪来。

Mother's Bible

母亲的圣经

Anonymous/佚名

For 12 years after my father died, my mother lived on alone in their little house with its roses. Then one day, when she was 84 after serving lunch to my two brothers, who often popped in for a bite, she hung her apron behind the door and went to join dad.

I wish this was all as idyllic as it sounds. She had not been feeling well for weeks, and I'm sure she sensed that she was going. She had made quite a few preparations, including leaving handwritten instructions in the small Bible she always used, where we'd be sure to find them. The one thing uppermost in her mind, however, was something she had been able to do little about. Two members of the family had been feuding — one of those agonizing conflicts between grown children that tear a parent apart. She had wept over it, prayed over it, but the wounds were far from healed.

在父亲去世后的12年里，母亲独自一人依旧住在他们原先所种的有玫瑰花的小房子里。她84岁时的一天，母亲给我两个经常回家吃饭的兄弟端上了午饭，把围裙挂到门后面，就与父亲团聚去了。

但愿这件事就像听起来那样富于诗意。几个星期以来，母亲一直感觉不太好，我相信她自己也觉得自己将不久于人世。她为此作了好多准备，包括把手写的临终嘱咐夹在她一直使用的那本小《圣经》中。我们肯定会在那儿找到它的。然而，母亲认为最主要的事情，却是她始终都无力去做的事情：孩子们中有两人一直不和，这是子女成年后，他们之间发生的使人痛苦，令父母撕心裂肺的冲突之一。母亲为此流过泪，祈祷过，但他们之间的创伤却远未愈合。

Now that the house was silent, the troubles seemed forgotten. There was so much to be done that there was simply no time for hostilities. Yet, even in the face of death, the problem refused to vanish altogether. Proprieties were maintained; even an extra show of courtesy was extended. But after that first surge of emotion, the tension resurfaced.

Then, that second night, we saw mother's heavy old family Bible on the table by the bookcase. Filled with records, that Bible had long ago been relegated to the top shelf of the bookcase. Yet here it lay, on a table that had been cleared and dusted! Who had taken it down? Mystified, we consulted with one another. No one else had been there. Each of us was as puzzled as the next. The Bible had simply appeared; there was no explanation for it.

Without a word everyone sat down, and my sister opened the book at its marker. She began to read from John 13:

"Now before the feast of the Passover, when Jesus knew that his hour was come that he should depart out of this world unto the Father, having loved his own which were in the world, he loved them unto the end."

She paused and looked around. All our eyes were wet. "And then there's this," she said, "this place is also marked."

"Little children, yet a little while I am with you. Ye shall seek me: and as I said unto the Jews, whither I go, ye cannot come; so now I say to you. A new commandment I give unto, that ye love one another; as I have told you, that ye also love one another."

She couldn't go on. She didn't have to. The two who had been feuding groped for each other's hands. Then they embraced, holding one to the other as if never to let go.

The peace they made that night was to last. Mother's passing had spanned their estrangement. The bridge of death had become the bridge of love.

母亲已去，屋内静寂无声，各种烦恼似乎也已被忘记。我们要做的事情太多，实在没有时间来打架。然而，即便面对母亲去世，两人间的不和依旧无法完全消除。开始，各人都保持了必要的礼貌，甚至相互间还格外客气。可是，在最初的客气过后，紧张的气氛又出现了。

接着，在第二天晚上，我们看到母亲那本旧的、厚厚的家用《圣经》就放在书橱旁边的桌子上。这本《圣经》，因为里面记满了东西，早已被放在书橱顶层不再使用了。可它今晚就在桌子上，桌子还擦拭得干干净净！是谁把它从书橱顶上拿下来的？我们感到奇怪，互相询问着。谁也没有到过那儿。我们全都疑惑不解。这本《圣经》确实又出现了，没有人知道这是怎么一回事。

我们都默默地坐下，姐姐翻到放书签处，从《约翰福音》的第13章第1节开始诵读：

“在逾越节的盛会前，耶稣知道他离开人间返回圣父身边的时刻就要到了，他爱他在世间的门徒们，就将他们爱到底。”

姐姐停顿下来，环视了一下周围。我们眼里都含着泪水。“还有这儿，”她说：“这儿也作了标记。”

“孩子们，我和你们在一起的时间不长了。你们会寻找我的：正如我对犹太人所说的，我去的地方，你们不能来。因此，我要对你们说，我要给你们下一条新命令，那就是你们要互相友爱，而且还要向我嘱咐的那样互相友爱。”

姐姐读不下去了，她也没有再往下读的必要了。一直不合的两个人试探着把手伸向对方。接着，他们紧紧地拥抱，仿佛永世都不再分离。

那晚他们的和解将继续到永远。母亲的去世弥合了他们的疏远，母亲的去世架起了家人友爱的桥梁。

A Coke and a Smile

可乐与微笑

Anonymous/佚名

I know now that the man who sat with me on the old wooden stairs that hot summer night over thirty-five years ago was not a tall man. But to a five-year-old, he was a giant. We sat side by side, watching the sun go down behind the old Texaco service station across the busy street. A street that I was never allowed to cross unless accompanied by an adult, or at the very least, an older sibling.

Cherry-scented smoke from Grampy's pipe kept the hungry mosquitoes at bay while gray, wispy swirls danced around our heads. Now and again, he blew a smoke ring and laughed as I tried to target the hole with my finger. I, clad in a cool summer nightie, and Grampy, his sleeveless T-shirt, sat watching the traffic. We counted cars and tried to guess the color of the next one to turn the corner.

我现在知道，在35年前那个炎热的夏夜，同我一起坐在破旧的木楼梯上的老人并不高大，但对一个5岁孩子来说，他却是一个巨人。我们并排坐着，看着太阳落在繁忙的街对面那个老得克萨斯加油站的背后。除非有大人或至少一个哥哥或姐姐陪着，我从未被允许穿过那条街。

从祖父烟斗里喷出的白色烟雾在我们脑袋周围上下旋绕，它们散发的樱桃香味使贪婪的蚊子不敢靠近。他不时地喷出一串烟圈，在我试着将手指插入烟圈时他放声大笑。我穿着凉爽的小睡衣，祖父穿着他的无袖T恤衫，坐在那儿观看繁忙的交通。我们数着过往的车辆，并猜想着下一辆拐过街角的汽车的颜色。

Once again, I was caught in the middle of circumstances. The fourth born of six children, it was not uncommon that I was either too young or too old for something. This night I was both. While my two baby brothers slept inside the house, my three older siblings played with friends around the corner, where I was not allowed to go. I stayed with Grampy, and that was okay with me. I was where I wanted to be. My grandfather was baby-sitting while my mother, father and grandmother went out.

"Thirsty?" Grampy asked, never removing the pipe from his mouth.

"Yes," was my reply. "How would you like to run over to the gas station there and get yourself a bottle of Coke?"

I couldn't believe my ears. Had I heard right? Was he talking to me? On my family's modest income, Coke was not a part of our budget or diet. A few tantalizing sips was all I had ever had, and certainly never my own bottle.

我又一次陷于两头都够不上的中间境遇，作为6个孩子中的老四，很多事情对于我来说不是因为年龄太小，就是因为年龄太大而不合适。那天夜里就是这样。我的两个小兄弟在屋里睡觉，我的另外3个长兄和姐姐在拐角与小伙伴们玩，而我是不允许去那里的。我与祖父呆在一起，这也挺好，正是我想呆的地方。在父母和祖母外出时，祖父就在家看孩子。

"渴吗?"祖父叼着烟斗问我。

"渴。"我回答说。"跑到街对面的加油站去给你自己买瓶可乐怎么样?"

我简直不敢相信自己的耳朵，我没有听错吧？他是在跟我说话吗？就我们家微薄的收入来说，可乐不是我们家庭开销的一部分。我只是嘬过几小口，从来没有自己喝过一瓶。

“Okay,” I replied shyly, already wondering how I would get across the street. Surely Grampy was going to come with me.

Grampy stretched his long leg out straight and reached his huge hand deep into the pocket. I could hear the familiar jangling of the loose change he always carried. Opening his fist, he exposed a mound of silver coins. There must have been a million dollars there. He instructed me to pick out a dime. After he deposited the rest of the change back into his pocket, he stood up.

“Okay,” he said, helping me down the stairs and to the curb, “I'm going to stay here and keep an ear out for the babies. I'll tell you when it's safe to cross. You go over to the Coke machine, get your Coke and come back out. Wait for me to tell you when it's safe to cross back.”

My heart pounded. I clutched my dime tightly in my sweaty palm. Excitement took my breath away.

“好的。”我害羞地回答说，心里在想着该怎样穿过马路，祖父当然会跟我一块。

祖父将他的长腿伸直，把他的大手伸进口袋。我能听到零钱相碰而发出的熟悉的叮□当声，他总是把这些零钱带在身上。他张开手，露出了一堆宝贝似的银币。那里面一定有100万美元！他让我拿出一个10美分的硬币。把零钱放回口袋后，他站了起来。

“好吧，”他说，帮着我下楼梯到马路沿儿那儿去，“我站在这儿，听着屋里的两个孩子有没有动静，什么时候穿过马路安全，我会告诉你的。你到对面的可乐机那儿买到你的可乐后再走回来。等着我告诉你什么时候过马路安全。”

我的心怦怦地跳着，紧紧地用汗手攥着那一枚10美分的硬币，兴奋得喘不上气来。

Grampy held my hand tightly. Together we looked up the street and down, and back up again. He stepped off the curb and told me it was safe to cross. He let go of my hand and I ran. I ran faster than I had ever run before. The street seemed wide. I wondered if I would make it to the other side. Reaching the other side, I turned to find Grampy. There he was, standing exactly where I had left him, smiling proudly. I waved.

"Go on, hurry up," he yelled.

My heart pounded wildly as I walked inside the dark garage. I had been inside the garage before with my father. My surroundings were familiar. I heard the Coca-Cola machine motor humming even before I saw it. I walked directly to the big old red-and-white dispenser. I knew where to insert my dime. I had seen it done before and had fantasized about this moment many times.

The big old monster greedily accepted my dime, and I heard the bottles shift. On tiptoes I reached up and opened the heavy door. There they were: one neat row of thick green bottles, necks staring directly at me, and ice cold from the refrigeration. I held the door open with my shoulder and grabbed one. With a quick yank, I pulled it free from its bondage. Another one immediately took its place. The bottle was cold in my sweaty hands. I will never forget the feeling of the cool glass on my skin. With two hands, I positioned the bottleneck under the heavy brass opener that was bolted to the wall. The cap dropped into an old wooden box, and I reached in to retrieve it. I was cold and bent in the middle, but I knew I needed to have this souvenir. Coke in hand, I proudly marched back out into the early evening dusk. Grampy was waiting patiently. He smiled.

"Stop right there," he yelled. One or two cars sped by me, and once again, Grampy stepped off the curb. "Come on, now," he said, "run." I did. Cool brown foam sprayed my hands. "Don't ever do that alone," he warned. I held the Coke bottle tightly, fearful he would make me pour it into a cup, ruining this dream come true. He didn't. One long swallow of the cold beverage cooled my sweating body. I don't think I ever felt so proud.

祖父紧紧地拉着我的手，我们一块儿看了看大街的前后左右。他走下马路沿儿，告诉我现在可以过去了。他放开我的手，我跑了起来。我从没有跑得这么快过。街道似乎很宽，我怀疑自己是否能跑到对面。跑到对面后，我回头寻找祖父，他正站在我离开他的地方，为我自豪地微笑着。我朝他挥了挥手。

“接着走，快点。”他喊道。

我的心怦怦乱跳着走进昏暗的修车站。我以前曾和父亲一块儿来过这里，对周围的一切都很熟悉。甚至在看见可口可乐机之前就听到了其马达发出的嗡嗡声。我径直走向那台红白相间的巨大的老自动售货机。我知道该往哪儿插硬币，我曾看过并曾多次幻想有一天我也能亲身试一试。

那个老巨人贪婪地吞下我的硬币，我听见了瓶子移动的声音。我踮起脚尖伸手摸索着打开了它厚重的门。它们就在那儿！一排整齐的深绿色瓶子，瓶颈一个挨一个地凝视着我，冰箱里散发出冰冷的气息。我用肩膀顶着门，伸手抓住一个，迅速一拉，将它从捆绑中拉了出来，另一个立即占据了它的位置。瓶子在我汗津津的手中显得格外冰凉，我永远忘不了冰凉的瓶子接触我皮肤时的感觉。我两手抓住瓶子，将瓶颈放在固定的厚铜开瓶器下，瓶盖立即掉在一个老木箱里，我伸手将它捡了出来，感觉好凉，中间已经弯曲，但我知道我需要拥有这个纪念品。手拿可乐，我自豪地走回到外面，已是黄昏时分。祖父正耐心地等待着，并面带微笑。

“停在那儿，”一两辆车在我面前飞驶而过，祖父再次走下马路沿儿，“现在过来”他说，“跑过来！”我跑了起来，冰凉的棕色泡沫溅在我的手上。“以后别再一个人独自过马路！”他警告我。我紧紧地抱着可乐瓶，生怕他让我把可乐倒在杯子里，毁掉我的梦想。他没有。我咕噜噜长长地吞下一口冰凉的可乐，冒汗的身体顿觉清爽无比。我认为自己从来没有过当时那样的自豪。

The Scar

伤疤

Anonymous/佚名

A little boy invited his mother to attend his elementary school's first teacher-parent conference. To the little boy's dismay, she said she would go. This would be the first time that his classmates and teacher met his mother and he was embarrassed by her appearance. Although she was a beautiful woman, there was a severe scar that covered nearly the entire right side of her face. The boy never wanted to talk about why or how she got the scar.

At the conference, the people were impressed by the kindness and natural beauty of his mother despite the scar, but the little boy was still embarrassed and hid himself from everyone. He did, however, get within earshot of a conversation between his mother and his teacher, and heard them speaking.

"How did you get the scar on your face?" the teacher asked.

有个小男孩邀请他的母亲去参加学校举办的第一次家长会。令他沮丧的事，妈妈竟然答应去。同学们和老师将是第一次见到妈妈，但是，妈妈的相貌令他感到难堪。虽然母亲非常漂亮，但她整个右脸几乎被一块严重的伤疤覆盖了。小男孩从来不曾想问母亲伤疤的来历。

家长会上，小男孩妈妈的善良和蔼以及天生丽质给人们留下了深刻的印象，没有人在意她脸上的那块伤疤。但是，小男孩却感到局促不安，他藏起来不与人打照面。尽管如此，他还是能听到妈妈和老师的谈话，能听见他们谈话的内容。

"您脸上的伤疤是怎么来的?"老师问道。

The mother replied, "When my son was a baby, he was in a room that caught on fire. Everyone was too afraid to go in because the fire was out of control, so I went in. As I was running toward his crib, I saw a beam coming down and I placed myself over him trying to protect him. I was knocked unconscious but fortunately, a fireman came in and saved both of us." She touched the burned side of her face. "This sear will be permanent, but to this day, I have never regretted doing what I did."

At this point, the little boy came out running towards his mother with tears in his eyes. He hugged her and felt an overwhelming sense of the sacrifice that his mother had made for him. He held her hand tightly for the rest of the day.

小男孩的妈妈答道："儿子很小的时候，他的房间突然着火了。大家都不敢进去，因为火势失控了。我进去了。就在我跑向他的婴儿床时，我看到一根房梁就要倒下来了，我扑到他的床上，想护住他。房梁把我砸晕了。幸运的是，消防员冲了进来，救了我们。"她摸着脸上的伤疤，说："这块伤疤会永远留在脸上，但是直到今天，我从没为我做的事后悔过。"

听到这里，小男孩走了出来，满含热泪奔向妈妈，拥抱着她。母亲为自己作出的牺牲让他内心激动无比。那天后来，小男孩一直紧紧地抓着妈妈的手。

The Champa Flower

金色花

Tagore/ 泰戈尔

Supposing I became a champa flower, just for fun, and grew on a branch high up that tree, and shook in the wind with laughter and danced upon the newly budded leaves, would you know me, mother?

You would call, "Baby, where are you?" and I should laugh to myself and keep quite quiet.

I should slyly open my petals and watch you at your work.

When after your bath, with wet hair spread on your shoulders, you walked through the shadow of the champa tree to the little court where you say you prayers, you would notice the scent of the flower, but not know that it came from me.

如果我变成一朵金色花——只是为了好玩，长在高高的枝头，在风中摇摆欢笑，在新绽的嫩叶上跳舞，你会知道那是我吗，妈妈？

你会叫着："孩子，你在哪里？"我会偷偷地笑，一句话也不说。

我会悄悄地张开我的花瓣，看你工作。

当你沐浴过后，湿湿的头发披散在双肩，你穿过金色花的树影走向你祈祷的小院，你会闻到金色花的花香，但你不会知道这芳香是从我身上散发的。

When after the midday meal you sat at the window reading *Ramayana*, and the tree's shadow fell over your hair and your lap, I should fling my wee little shadow on to the page of your book, just where you were reading.

But would you guess that it was the tiny shadow of your little child?

When in the evening you went to the cow-shed with the lighted lamp in your hand, I should suddenly drop on to the earth again and be your own baby once more, and beg you to tell me a story.

"Where have you been, you naughty child?"

"I won't tell you, mother." That's what you and I would say then.

吃过午饭，你坐在窗前读《罗摩衍那》，树荫拂过你的头发和双膝，我将我小小的花影投射到你的书页上，那恰是你正读着的地方。

但是你能猜到这个小小的影子是你小小的孩子吗?

当夜晚来临，你手里提着灯去牛棚，我会突然跳到地上，再次变成你的小孩子，要求你给我讲个故事。

"淘气的孩子，你跑到哪里去了呢?"

"我不告诉你，妈妈。"这就是你我那时要说的话了。

Outside Looking in

窗内

Anonymous/佚名

I step out the back door and the blackness of night engulfs me. There is no moon to light my way to the clothes-line and my forgotten wash. I'm piloted by the memory of a thousand trips along the familiar path: now up two flag-stone steps, now past the giant pine whose branches overhang our cottage.

Past the corner of the woodshed, my out stretched hands become my scouts, groping for the lines, fumbling with the pins. Soon my arms are heaped with night-damp pants and shirts that have danced all day to the wind's compelling tunes.

The trip back is easier. The lights of the house guide me — great squares of amber light suspended in the darkness. The moment my gaze penetrates the glass, I become suspended too.

Everything inside the house appears transformed. The kitchen cabinets look warmer, richer, the rows of spices and jars and bottles are homier. Even the pine wall behind the stove, so utilitarian with hanging pots, glows with a new personality.

一走出后门，黑夜就吞没了我。没有月光的照耀，我摸黑走向晾衣绳，去取忘记收回的衣服。这条路我走了有一千次了，熟得凭着记忆就能够知道自己应该踏上两级石板阶梯，再经过那株把树枝一直伸到我们屋顶的巨大松树。

经过木棚的拐角，我伸手摸索着晾衣绳，取下衣夹。很快我的胳膊就搭满了被夜雾弄湿的衣裤，它们已经被风吹舞了一天。

回去就简单多了。屋里的灯光指引着我——那些在黑暗中发亮的大方块。当我向玻璃窗里面望进去的时候，我的心一下子就像是悬空了。

屋子里面的一切仿佛都变了。厨房里的橱柜变得更加温馨，更富足：成排的香料、瓶子、壶，甚至炉子后面挂着的锅的松木板墙，都有了新的面貌。

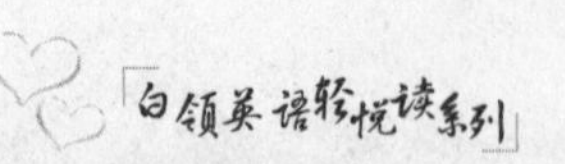

I back up farther into the yard. From here I can see the living room. John's head is bent over a spelling book, his hair golden in the lamplight, his face set with a frown of concentration. Robert kneels by the Sofa, pushing a wheeled Lego contraption along the cliff-edge of the cushion. The corner of a newspaper flaps into sight and disappears as Richard's invisible hands turn the pages. I picture his absorbed face, studious-looking in new reading glasses.

Colored as they are with a rich topaz light, these ordinary scenes now seem imbued with vibrancy and charm, which flow not so much from the lamps as from the feelings of warmth and peace they inspire. For a split second I am a stranger peeking into a home I have never seen before.

I ask myself, what if I really became a stranger? What if I could never get back into these rooms? What if I could never again touch John's springy hair or see Robert's guileless smile?

我往院子深处再退一点，从那里能够看到客厅。约翰低着头，正在看一本识字课本，他的头发在灯光下变成了金色，他的眉头因为集中注意力而皱在一起。罗伯特在沙发上，跪着用手推一个积木搭成的小车，在垫子边上移动。理查德在看报纸，我看不到他的手，只能时不时看到报纸角。我能想象他戴着老花镜认真看报的样子。

在金黄色的灯光照耀下，平凡的情景变得充满魅力，充满温馨和宁静。一瞬间我仿佛变成了一个外人，正在偷窥一个陌生的家庭。

我问我自己，如果我真的是一个陌生人怎么办？如果再也不能抚摸约翰弯曲的头发，再也不能看到罗伯特天真的笑脸，该怎么办？

Deep inside me, a door opens that barrier we set up to guard our secret selves and without conditions I let my family in. All the annoyances that families are prone to, all the kinks and stumbling blocks in our relationships, all the difficulties of living together in barmony become trivial — over-whelmed by the simple fact that we love one another.

Moments like this don't occur every day, and maybe that's the way it should be. It would be exhausting to live our lives weighed down by such intensity of feeling. But the memory sustains me, just as the smell of fresh air clings to the clothes in my arms. Tomorrow morning when I slip them on, my armor against the world, the lingering fragrance will remind me that they have danced in the darkness, under the pines, on the edge of a deep, golden light.

在我内心深处，一扇门开了，一道专为存放内心感受而设计的屏障打开了，我无条件地让我的家人进入。每个家庭都有苦恼，家人之间的种种不愉快，让家人不能自在地生活在一起的问题，在“我们相亲相爱”的事实面前都显得微不足道。

这样的时刻不会每天都有，也许事情就是这样。如果我们总是情感激烈，那可能会因为很累而受不了。但是这样的记忆会永远伴随着我，让我充满勇气和信心，就像我臂弯上那些衣服的清新气息。明天早上当我穿上这些衣服的时候，残留的香气会让我回忆起它们曾在松树下，在黑暗里、金黄色灯光的边缘起舞。

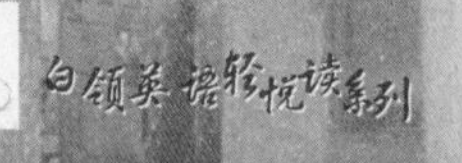

A Mother's Letter to the World

一位母亲写给世界的信

Anne Stone/ 安妮·斯通

Dear World:

My son starts school today. It's going to be strange and new to him for a while. And I wish you would sort of treat him gently.

You see, up to now, he's been king of the roost. He's been boss of the back yard. I have always been around to repair his wounds, and to soothe his feelings.

But now — things are going to be different.

This morning, he's going to walk down the front steps, wave his hand and start on his great adventure that will probably include wars and tragedy and sorrow. To live his life in the world he has to live in will require faith and love and courage.

亲爱的世界：

我的儿子今天要开始上学读书了。一时之间，他会感觉陌生而又新鲜。而我希望你能待他温柔一些。

你明白，到现在为止，他一直是家中的小皇帝；一直是后院的王者。我一直在他身旁，忙着为他治疗伤口，并慰藉他的心情。

但是现在——一切都将不同了。

今天清晨，他就要走下前门的楼梯，冲我挥挥手，开始他的伟大的历险征程，其间或许有争斗、不幸或者伤痛。要在这个世界上生存度日，他需要信念、爱心和勇气。

So, World, I wish you would sort of take him by his young hand and teach him the things he will have to know. Teach him — but gently, if you can. Teach him that for every scoundrel, there is a hero; that for every crooked politician there is a dedicated leader; that for every enemy there is a friend. Teach him the wonders of books. Give him quiet time to ponder the eternal mystery of birds in the sky, bees in the sun, and flowers on the green hill. Teach him it is far more honorable to fail than to cheat. Teach him to have faith in his own ideas, even if everyone else tells him they are wrong. Teach him to sell his brawn and brains to the highest bidder, but never to put a price on his heart and soul. Teach him to close his ears to a howling mob and to stand and fight if he thinks he's right. Teach him gently, World, but don't coddle him, because only the test of fire makes fine steel.

This is a big order, World, but see what you can do. He's such a nice little fellow.

所以，世界啊，我希望你能够时不时握住他稚嫩的小手，教育他所应当知晓的事情。教育他吧——而如果可能的话，温柔一些。教他知道，每有恶人之地，必有豪杰所在；每有奸诈小人，必有献身义士；每见一敌人，必有一友在侧。教他感受书本的神奇魅力。给他时间静思大自然中亘古绵传之奥秘：空中的飞鸟，日光里的蜜蜂，青山上的簇簇繁花。教他知道，失败远比欺骗更为光荣；教他坚定自我的信念，哪怕人人予以否认；教他可以最高价付出自己的精力和智慧，但绝不可出卖良心和灵魂；教他置群氓的喧嚣于度外……并在自觉正确之时挺身而战。温柔地教导他吧，世界，但是不要放纵他。因为只有烈火的考验才能炼出真钢。

这一要求甚高，世界，但是请尽你所能。他是一个如此可爱的小家伙。

Christmas Star

圣诞星

Anonymous/佚名

This was my grandmother's first Christmas without grandfather, and we had promised him before he passed away that we would make this her best Christmas ever. When my mom, dad, three sisters and I arrived at her little house in the Blue Ridge Mountains of North Carolina, we found she had waited up all night for us to arrive from Texas. After we exchanged hugs, my sisters and I ran into the house. It did seem a little empty without grandfather, and we knew it was up to us to make this Christmas special for her.

Grandfather had always said that the Christmas tree was the most important decoration of all. So we immediately set to work on the beautiful artificial tree that was kept stored in grandfather's closet. Although artificial, it was the most genuine looking Christmas tree I had ever seen. Tucked away in the closet with the tree was a spectacular array of ornaments, many of which had been my father's when he was a little boy. As we unwrapped each one, grandmother had a story to go along with it. My mother strung the tree with bright white lights and a red button garland; my sisters and I carefully placed the ornaments on the tree; and finally father was given the honor of lighting the tree.

We stepped back to admire our handiwork. To us, it look led magnificent, as beautiful as the tree in Rockefeller Center. But something was missing.

这是奶奶第一个没有爷爷的圣诞节，我们在他去世前答应过他，我们要让她过一个最好的圣诞节。当爸爸、妈妈、我和3个姐姐抵达位于北卡罗来纳蓝脊山奶奶的小房子时，我们发现她整晚没睡，等着我们从得克萨斯过去。相互拥抱过后我和姐妹们都跑进了屋子。没有了爷爷，屋子看上去确实显得空荡荡的。我们知道该由我们来让奶奶度过一个特别的圣诞。

爷爷总是说圣诞树是圣诞节里最重要的装饰。所以我们立刻着手开始装扮那棵爷爷放在储存柜里的漂亮的人造树。虽然是人造的，但它是我所见过最仿真的圣诞树，和圣诞树一起放在柜子里的还有一排饰物，很多是爸爸小的时候就有了的。我们每打开一件东西，奶奶都要告诉我们它的故事。妈妈用明亮的白色小灯和一个用红色扣形花环把圣诞树串起来，我和姐妹们把饰物挂上圣诞树。爸爸拥有最后的荣幸负责点亮圣诞树。

我们往后站站欣赏着我们的杰作，对我们来说它是那么的华丽，就和洛克菲勒购物中心的树一样漂亮，但是好像缺点儿什么？

"Where's your star" I asked.

The star was my grandmother's favorite part of the tree, for it represented the star of Bethlehem that had led the wise men to the infant Jesus.

"Why, it must be here somewhere," she said, starting to sort through the boxes again. "Your grandfather always packed everything so carefully when he took the tree down."

我问奶奶："您的星星呢?"

星星是圣诞树上奶奶最喜欢的部分，因为它代表着伯利恒之星指引智者走向婴儿耶稣。

"奇怪，肯定在这儿的某个地方，"她说，然后开始在盒子里搜寻，"你爷爷总是很仔细地把每件东西打包，然后拆下圣诞树。"

As we emptied box after box and found no star, my grandmother's eyes filled with tears. This was no ordinary ornament, but an elaborate golden star covered with colored jewels and blue lights that blinked on and off. Moreover, grandfather had given it to grandmother some fifty years ago on their first Christmas together. Now, on her first Christmas without him, the star was gone, too.

"Don't worry, Grandmother," I reassured her. "We'll find it for you."

My sisters and I formed a search party.

"Let's start in on the closet where the ornaments were," Donna said. "Maybe the box just fell down."

That sounded logical, so we climbed on a chair and began to search that tall closet of grandfather's. We found grandfather's old yearbooks and photographs of relatives, Christmas cards from years gone by and party dresses and jewelry boxes, but no star.

当我们把盒子一个个倒空来找时，奶奶的眼睛里满是泪水。这不是一般的饰品，而是一颗精美无比的金色星星，覆盖着彩色的亮珠和可以一闪一闪的蓝色小灯。并且它是50年前，爷爷奶奶一起过第一个圣诞节时爷爷送给奶奶的，现在，在她第一个没有爷爷的圣诞节，星星也不见了。

“别担心，奶奶，我们会帮您找到的。”我安慰着她。

我和姐妹们组成了一支搜索队。

“我们从放饰物的柜子开始找起吧，”唐纳说，“可能盒子正好掉下来了。”

听上去很有道理，于是我们爬上凳子开始翻爷爷那个高柜子，我们找到了爷爷的老年鉴和一些亲戚的相片，一些多年前的圣诞卡，舞会的衣服，还有珠宝盒子，但就是没有那颗星星。

We searched under beds and over shelves, inside and outside, until we had exhausted every possibility. We could see grandmother was disappointed, although she tried not to show it.

"We could buy a new star," Kristi offered.

"I'll make you one from construction paper," Karen chimed in.

"No," Grandmother said. "This year, we won't have a star."

By now, it was dark outside, and time for bed, since Santa would soon be here. As we lay in bed, we could hear the sound of snowflakes falling quietly outside.

The next morning, my sisters and I woke up early, as was our habit on Christmas day-first, to see what Santa had left under the tree, and second, to look for the Christmas star in the sky. After a traditional breakfast of apple pancakes, the family sat down together to open presents. Santa had brought me the Easy Bake Oven I wanted, and Donna a Chatty Cathy doll. Karen was thrilled to get the doll buggy she had asked for, and Kristi to get the china tea set. Father was in charge of passing out the presents, so that everyone would have something to open at the same time.

我们把床底下、架子上里里外外找了个遍，每一种可能都被排除了。尽管奶奶尽量不表现出来，我们还是看得出她很失望。

克里斯蒂提议说："我们可以买个新的。"

凯伦插嘴说："我可以用彩纸重做一个。"

可奶奶说："不，今年我们不用星星了。"

现在外面漆黑一片，该上床睡觉了，也许圣诞老人很快就要来到。我们躺在床上听见外面雪花飘落的声音。

第二天一大早，我们很早就起了，这是我们家圣诞节的传统。首先看看圣诞老人在圣诞树下放了什么礼物，接着找寻天空中的圣诞星。吃完传统的苹果薄饼早餐后，一家人坐在一起拆礼物。圣诞老人送给我一个我一直想要的简易烤箱，唐纳得了一个会说话的洋娃娃。凯伦收到一个梦寐以求的玩具车，兴奋极了。克里斯蒂得到了一套瓷器茶具。爸爸负责发礼物，让每个人都能同时拆看。

“The last gift is to Grandmother from Grandfather,” he said, in a puzzled voice.

“From who?” There was surprise in my grandmother’s voice.

“I found that gift in grandfather’s closet when we got the tree down,” mother explained. “It was already wrapped so I put it under the tree. I thought it was one of yours.”

“Hurry and open it,” Karen urged excitedly.

My grandmother shakily opened the box. Her face lit up with joy when she unfolded the tissue paper and pulled out a glorious golden star. There was a note attached. Her voice trembled as she read it aloud.

“Don’t be angry with me, dear. I broke your star while putting up the decorations, and I couldn’t bear to tell you. I thought it was time for a new one. I hope it brings you as much joy as the first one. Merry Christmas.

Love, Bryant.”

So grandmother’s tree had a star after all, a star that expressed their everlasting love for one another. It brought my grandfather home for Christmas in each of our hearts and made it our best Christmas ever.

爸爸困惑地说：“最后一件礼物是爷爷送给奶奶的。”

“谁送的？”奶奶的声音充满了惊奇。

“我们把圣诞树拿下来时，我在爷爷的柜子里出现了这个礼物，”妈妈解释道，“它已经包好了，所以我把它放到了圣诞树下，我想可能是给你的礼物。”

凯伦激动地催促道：“快打开看看。”

奶奶颤抖着打开那个盒子，当她打开包装纸拿出一个金光闪闪的星星时，她的脸似乎突然被快乐点亮起来。上面附了一张便条，她用微抖的声音读了出来，

“亲爱的，别生我的气，我在装饰品时打碎了你的星星。我不敢告诉你，我想是该换个新的时候了。希望这一个能带给你和第一个同样的快乐。圣诞快乐

爱你的布莱恩特”

最终奶奶的圣诞树有了一颗星星，一颗代表着他们之间永恒爱情的星星。它在圣诞节时分将爷爷带回了家里，带到我们每个人心里，今年的节日成为我们最好的一个圣诞节。

A Box Full of Kisses

亲亲满匣飞

Anonymous/佚名

The story goes that some time ago, a man punished his 3-year-old daughter for wasting a roll of gold wrapping paper. Money was tight and he became infuriated when the child tried to decorate a box to put under the Christmas tree. Nevertheless, the little girl brought the gift to her father the next morning and said, "This is for you, Daddy."

The man was embarrassed by his earlier overreaction, but his anger flared again when he found out the box was empty. He yelled at her, stating, "Don't you know, when you give someone a present, there is supposed to be something inside?" The little girl looked up at him with tears in her eyes and cried, "Oh, Daddy, it's not empty at all. I blew kisses into the box. They're all for you, Daddy."

The father was crushed. He put his arms around his little girl, and he begged for her forgiveness.

Only a short time later, an accident took the life of the child. It is also told that her father kept that gold box by his bed for many years and, whenever he was discouraged, he would take out an imaginary kiss and remember the love of the child who had put it there.

Each one of us, as human beings, has been given a gold container filled with unconditional love and kisses from our children, family members and friends. There is simply no other possession, anyone could hold, more precious than this.

这个故事说的是以前，一个男子惩罚了他 3 岁的女儿，因为她浪费了一卷金箔包装纸。家里经济困难，当他知道女儿包了一个盒子放在圣诞树下时，他简直怒气冲天。但第二天，女儿把礼物拿到他面前说：“爸爸，这是给你的。”

爸爸为前一天晚上的举动感到羞愧难当，但是当他发现盒子里什么都没装时，他再一次暴怒，对着女儿大吼道：“莫非你不知道当你送别人礼物时，你要放东西进去吗?”女儿抬起脸看着他，眼眶里满是泪水，边哭边说：“哦，爸爸，那不是空盒子。我飞了好多好多个亲吻进去，都是给你的。”

爸爸惊呆了，他拥抱着女儿，祈求她的原谅。

不久以后，女儿在一次事故中丧生。爸爸一直把那个金盒子放在床畔，放了很多很多年。每当心情沮丧时，他就拿出一个想象中的亲吻，想念着那个将吻吹进了盒子的孩子给他的爱。

我们每一个人都有一个金罐子，里面装满了无条件的爱和吻，有孩子的，有家人的，还有朋友的。没有人可以拥有比这个更加珍贵的财产。

Embassy of Hope

希望大使馆

David Like

大卫·莱克

When Mark was five years old his parents divorced. He stayed with his mother, while his father enlisted in the armed forces. As Mark grew up he occasionally had recollections of the brief time he shared with his father and longed to one day see him again, but as Mark became an adult the thoughts of his father began to subside. Mark was now more into girls, motorcycles, and partying.

After Mark graduated from college he married his high school sweetheart. A year later she gave birth to a healthy bouncing baby boy.

One day when Mark's son was five years old and as Mark was preparing to shave his face, his son looked up at him and laughed, "Daddy you look like a clown with that whipped cream on your face."

马克5岁时父母离婚了。爸爸参了军，他和妈妈一起生活。马克成长中偶尔会想起他和爸爸一起度过的短暂时光，盼望着某一天能再见到爸爸。但当马克长大成人后，想爸爸的念头便烟消云散了，马克现在更多的是想女孩子、骑摩托车、参加聚会。

马克大学毕业后娶了他高中时的女友，1年后她生下了一个健康的小男孩。

儿子5岁的一天，他正准备刮胡子，儿子看着他笑起来，“爸爸脸上抹着泡泡，看上去像个小丑。”

Mark laughed, looked into the mirror and realized how much his son looked like him at that age. Later he remembered a story his mother had told him of him once telling his own father the same thing.

Mark began thinking about his own father a lot and started quizzing his mother. It had been a long time since Mark spoke of his father and his mother informed him that she had not spoken to his father in over twenty years and all her knowledge of his whereabouts ceased when Mark became eighteen.

Mark looked deep into his mother's eyes and said, "I need to find my father."

His mother commented that his relatives had all passed away and she had no idea where to begin searching for him but added, "Maybe, just maybe, if you contact the United States Embassy in England, they might be able to help you."

Even though the chances seemed slim Mark was determined. He called the Embassy and the conversation went something like this.

"U. S. Embassy, how may we help you?"

马克笑了，看着镜子，意识到这个年纪的儿子和自己那时有多像。后来，他想起妈妈给他讲过的他的一个故事，他有一次也对自己的爸爸说过同样的话。

马克开始想自己的爸爸，并不断问妈妈关于爸爸的事。妈妈告诉他，她已经有20多年没跟他父亲联系了，所有她知道的他的下落都消失于马克18岁那一年。

马克深深地望进母亲的双眸说："我要找爸爸。"

母亲说父亲所有的亲戚都去世了，她也不知该从哪里着手寻找，不过她补充了一句："可能，只是可能，如果你联系美国驻英国大使馆，或许他们能帮助你。"

尽管希望很渺茫，但马克心意已决。他给大使馆打了电话，谈话内容如下：

"美国大使馆，有什么能帮您吗？"

"Ahh hi, my name is Mark Sullivan and I am hoping to find my father."

After a long pause and the ruffle of papers "Is this a Mr. Mark Joseph Sullivan?"

"Yes," Mark says anxiously.

"And you were born in Vincennes, Indiana, at the Good Samaritan Hospital on October 19, 1970?"

"Yes, yes."

"Mark, please don't hang up." The man makes an announcement at the embassy. "Everyone listen I have terrific news Lieutenant Ronald L. Sullivan's son is on the phone he found us!"

Without a pause Mark hears a roar of a crowd clapping, cheering, laughing, crying, and praising God.

The man returns to the telephone and says, "Mark we're so glad you have called. Your father has been coming here in person or calling almost every single day for the past nine years, checking to see if we located you."

The following day Mark received a phone call from his father. His father explained to him that he had been traveling to the United States every six months trying to find him. Once even went to a home where the landlord had explained that Mark and his mother had moved out just two weeks prior and left no forwarding address.

Mark and his father now see each other as often as possible.

"啊，您好，我叫马克·沙立文，我希望能找到我父亲。"

对方停了很长一段时间，翻了一些文件然后说："请问是一位叫马克·约瑟·沙立文的先生吗？

"是的。"马克焦虑地说。

"您1970年10月9日出生于印第安纳州温森斯的古得·斯玛瑞藤医院吗？"

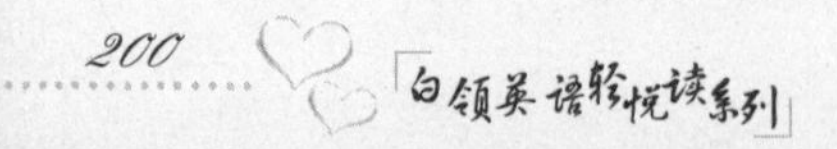

“是的，没错。”

“马克，请别挂电话。”那边那个男人在大使馆里广播道：“大家注意了，我有好消息，罗纳德沙立文中尉的儿子在电话那端，他找到了我们。”

瞬间，毫无迟疑，马克听见人群的欢呼声，人们鼓掌、喝彩、欢笑、喜极而泣，赞颂上帝。

那个男人回过来对他说：“马克，您给我们打电话，我们实在太高兴了。你父亲9年来每天都自己来或打电话过来问我们找到您没有。”

第二天，马克接到父亲的电话，父亲说，他每隔半年就会飞回去美国一次，想找到他。有一次甚至都找到他们曾经住过的地方，但房东告诉他，马克和他母亲两星期前才搬走，没有留下地址。

马克和他父亲现在尽可能多地彼此相见。

The Making of a Mother

上帝造母

Anonymous/佚名

By the time Lord made mothers, he was into the sixth day working overtime. An Angel appeared and said, "Why are you spending so much time on this one?"

And the Lord answered and said, "Have you read the spec sheet on her? She has to be completely washable, but not elastic; have 200 movable parts, all replaceable; run on black coffee and leftovers; have a lap that can hold three children at one time and that disappears when she stands up; have a kiss that can cure anything from a scraped knee to a broken heart; and have six pairs of hands."

The Angel was astounded at the requirements for this one. "Six pairs of hands! No way!" said the Angel.

上帝造母亲的时候，他已经没日没夜地连续干了6天了，一个天使现身过来问他："为什么这一个要花这么多时间？"

上帝答道："你没看见她上面贴的标签吗？她必须是百分之百可冲洗，但没有弹性不能伸缩拉长；有200个零件，每一个都可以替换；以黑咖啡和剩菜为生；坐下来时大腿上能一次放3个孩子，站起来就立刻恢复正常；她的吻可以治愈任何伤口，不管是膝盖上的小伤还是破碎的心灵；而且她还有6双手。"

听到这样的要求，天使大吃一惊。"6双手！那是不可能的。"天使说。

The Lord replied, "Oh, it's not the hands that are the problem. It's the three pairs of eyes that mothers must have!"

"And that's on the standard model?" the Angel asked.

The Lord nodded in agreement, "Yep, one pair of eyes are to see through the closed door as she asks her children what they are doing even though she already knows. Another pair in the back of her head are to see what she needs to know even though no one thinks she can. And the third pair are here in the front of her head. They are for looking at an errant child and saying that she understands and loves him or her without even saying a single word."

The Angel tried to stop the Lord "This is too much work for one day. Wait until tomorrow to finish."

"But I can't!" The Lord protested, "I am so close to finishing this creation that is so close to my own heart. She already heals herself when she is sick AND can feed a family of six on a pound of hamburger and can get a nine year old to stand in the shower."

上帝回答道："噢，有6双手还不算问题，关键是妈妈们都必须有3双眼睛。"

天使问："就是模特上的这样?"

上帝点点头，"是的，一双眼睛在询问孩子们在做什么时用来透视紧闭的房门，尽管她知道答案；后脑勺上长的用来看她该知道的事情，就算别人都觉得她不知道；第三双长在额头上，凝视犯了错的孩子，告诉孩子她懂他/她、爱他/她，不需要絮叨的言语。"

天使想让上帝停下来，说道："这么多活儿，一天干不完的，明天再干吧。"

"但我不想停!"上帝反对道，"就快要完成了，这个作品是那么接近我的内心所想。她已经能在生病时自动痊愈，并且能用一磅汉堡包喂饱一家6口，能让9岁的孩子乖乖洗澡。"

The Angel moved closer and touched the woman, "But you have made her so soft, Lord."

"She is soft," the Lord agreed, "but I have also made her tough. You have no idea what she can endure or accomplish."

"Will she be able to think?" asked the Angel.

The Lord replied, "Not only will she be able to think, she will be able to reason, and negotiate."

The Angel then noticed something and reached out and touched the woman's cheek. "Oops, it looks like you have a leak with this model. I told you that you were trying to put too much into this one."

"That's not a leak." The Lord objected. "That's a tear!"

"What's the tear for?" The Angel asked.

The Lord said, "The tear is her way of expressing her joy, her sorrow, her disappointment, her pain, her loneliness, her grief, and her pride."

The Angel was impressed. "You a genius, Lord. You thought of everything for this one. You even created the tear!"

The Lord looked at the Angel and smiled and said, "I'm afraid you are wrong again. I created the woman, but she created the tear!"

天使凑近点摸了摸这个女人，"但是上帝啊，你把她做得这么软。"

"她确实很柔软，"上帝表示赞同，"但我也把她做得很坚强。你不会知道她能忍耐和完成什么样的事情。"

"她能独立思考吗？"天使问。

上帝答道："她不仅能独立思考，而且她还会推理和磋商。"

天使注意到一些东西，他摸了摸女人的面颊，然后说："哦，看上去你的模特好像漏水了。我跟你说过，你在这一个上投入太多。"

上帝反对道："那不是漏水，那是一滴眼泪！"

天使问："眼泪是拿来做什么用的？"

上帝说："眼泪是她用来表达感情的，快乐、悲伤、失望、痛苦、孤独、忧郁以及骄傲。"

天使被打动了："上帝，你真是个天才。你为她设想了所有的事情，甚至给她造了眼泪。"

上帝望着天使，微笑着说道："恐怕你又错了。我创造了这个女人，而她创造了眼泪。"

Is Packaging Important to You?

形式很重要吗?

Anonymous/佚名

A young man was getting ready to graduate college. For many months he had admired a beautiful sports car in a dealer's showroom, and knowing his father could well afford it, he told him that was all he wanted.

As Graduation Day approached, the young man awaited signs that his father had purchased the car. Finally, on the morning of his graduation his father called him into his private study. His father told him how proud he was to have such a fine son, and told him how much he loved him. He handed his son a beautiful wrapped gift box.

Curious, but somewhat disappointed the young man opened the box and found a lovely, leather-bound Bible. Angrily, he raised his voice at his father and said, "With all your money you give me a Bible?" and stormed out of the house, leaving the holy book.

Many years passed and the young man was very successful in business. He had a beautiful home and wonderful family, but realized his father was very old, and thought perhaps he should go to him. He had not seen him since that graduation day. Before he could make arrangements, he received a telegram telling him his father had passed away, and willed all of his possessions to his son. He needed to come home immediately and take care things. When he arrived at his father's house, sudden sadness and regret filled his heart.

He began to search his father's important papers and saw the still new Bible, just as he had left it years ago. With tears, he opened the Bible and began to turn the pages. As he read those words, a car key dropped from an envelope taped behind the Bible. It had a tag with the dealer's name, the same dealer who had the sports car he had desired. On the tag was the date of his graduation, and the words…PAID IN FULL.

有一个年轻小伙子即将大学毕业，他在一个经销商的展室里看中一款跑车好几个月了，他知道他爸爸肯定买得起，于是告诉爸爸这就是他想要的。

毕业日终于到了，小伙子期盼着某些征兆暗示爸爸买了那款跑车。最后，毕业日清晨，爸爸把他叫进自己的书房，告诉他能拥有这样一个儿子，他是多么的骄傲，他有多么爱他。他递给儿子一个包装精美的礼品盒。

小伙子有点好奇，更多的是失望，他打开盒子，发现里面放着一本精美的皮面圣经。他很气愤，提高了嗓门儿对父亲嚷道："你那么多钱，却送一本圣经？"然后冲出门去，丢下了那本圣经。

很多年后，那个年轻小伙儿在事业上非常成功，有漂亮的房子和美满的家庭。儿子自从那年毕业典礼之后就在没见过父亲，他意识到父亲年事已高，自己应该去看看他。他还没有作出安排就收到了一封电报，上面说他父亲已经去世了，立下遗嘱将所有财产留给他。他必须马上回去料理所有事宜。当他抵达父亲家时，所有悲伤和悔恨都猛然袭上心头。

他开始整理父亲的一些重要文件，看见了那本当年他留下的仍然崭新的圣经。含着眼泪，他打开圣经一页页地翻阅。当他读着那些文字时，一把车钥匙从一个贴在圣经后面的信封里掉了下来，上面贴着经销商的名字，是以前他梦寐以求的那款跑车的经销商，标签上写着他毕业的日期，另外还有一行字"款已付清"。

The Son
《儿子》画像

Anonymous/佚名

A wealthy man and his son loved to collect rare works of art. They had everything in their collection, from Picasso to Raphael. They would often sit together and admire the great works of art.

When the Vietnam conflict broke out, the son went to war. He was very courageous and died in battle while rescuing another soldier. The father was notified and grieved deeply for his only son.

About a month later, just before Christmas, there was a knock at the door. A young man stood at the door with a large package in his hands. He said, "Sir, you don't know me, but I am the soldier for whom your son gave his life. He saved many lives that day, and he was carrying me to safety when a bullet struck him in the heart and he died instantly. He often talked about you, and your love for art."

一个富豪和他的儿子非常喜欢收藏稀有艺术品，他们的收藏品无所不包，从毕加索到拉斐尔，他们经常坐在一起欣赏这些伟大的艺术品。

越南战争爆发时，儿子参军了，他非常勇敢，一次战斗中在挽救同伴时牺牲了。爸爸得到消息后对失去唯一的爱子悲痛万分。

大约一个月以后，圣诞节前夕，有人敲门。门口站着的是一个年轻人，手里拿着一个很大的包裹，他说："先生，您不认识我，我就是您儿子救的那个士兵。那天他救了很多人的命，当他把我背到安全地带时一颗子弹射中了他的心脏，他当即牺牲了。他经常谈起您，谈及您对艺术的热爱。"

The young man held out his package.

"I know this isn't much. I'm not really a great artist, but I think your son would have wanted you to have this."

The father opened the package. It was a portrait of his son, painted by the young man. He stared in awe at the way the soldier had captured the personality of his son in the painting. The father was so drawn to the eyes that his own eyes welled up with tears. He thanked the young man and offered to pay him for the portrait.

"Oh, no sir, I could never repay what your son did for me. It's a gift."

The father hung the portrait over his mantle. Every time visitors came to his home he took them to see the portrait of his son before he showed them any of the other great works he had collected. The man died a few months later. There was to be a great auction of his painting. Many influential people purchase one for their collection. On the platform sat the painting of the son.

年轻人递上那个大包裹说：

“我知道这不值钱，我也不是什么杰出艺术家，但我想可能您儿子会希望您收下它。”

父亲打开包裹，是年轻人画的他儿子的肖像，当看到画家在画像里完全抓住了他儿子的神韵和个性特征时，他敬畏地注视着画像。父亲深深地沉浸在那双眸子里，自己也热泪盈眶。他谢过这年轻人，想向他买下这幅肖像。

“不，先生，您儿子给予我的东西，我永远无法回报，这是一个礼物。”

父亲将画像挂在壁炉架上方的墙上，每次有人来欣赏他所收藏的那些伟大的艺术品时，他都会先带他们来看他儿子的画像。这位富豪几个月后去世了，人们将对他的藏品举行一个大型的拍卖会。很多有权有势的人会为了他们的收藏买上一件。台子正中间放着儿子的画像。

The auctioneer pounded his gavel. "We will start the bidding with this portrait of the son. Who will bid for this painting?" There was silence. Then a voice in the back of the room shouted. "We want to see the famous paintings. Skip this one." But the auctioneer persisted. "Will someone bid for this painting? Who will start the biding? $100, $200?" Another voice shouted angrily. "We didn't come to see this painting. We came to see the Van Goghs, the Rembrandts. Get on with the real bids!" but still the auctioneer continued. "The Son! The Son! Who'll take The Son?"

Finally, a voice came from the very back of the room. It was the long-time gardener of the man and his son. "I'll give $10 for the painting." Being a poor man, it was all he could afford. "We have $10, who will bid $20?" "Give it to him for $10. Let's see the masters." "$10 is the bid, won't someone bid $20?"

竞拍师击槌开始。"我们将从儿子的画像开始，谁出价买这幅油画?"下面一片寂静，房间后面一个声音喊道："我们要看那些著名油画，把这幅跳过去吧。"但竞拍师坚持着，"谁愿出价买这幅画，谁愿开始投标? 100美元? 200美元?"另一个声音气愤地嚷着："我们可不是来看这个的。我们是来看梵·高、伦勃朗的，快开始真正的拍卖吧!"但竞拍师继续着，"《儿子》、《儿子》、谁买《儿子》?"

最后，一个声音从房间最后响起，是那个长年为富豪和儿子工作的花匠。"我出10美元买这幅画。"作为一个穷人，这是他所能出的最高价了。"10美元，有谁出20美元的?""10美元卖给他吧，快让我们看看那些大师的作品。""10美元竞标。有人出20美元吗?"

The crowd was becoming angry. They didn't want the painting of the son. They wanted the more worthy investments for their collections. The auctioneer pounded the gavel. "Going once, twice, SOLD for $10!" A man sitting on the second row shouted. "Now let's get on with the collection!"

The auctioneer laid down his gavel.

"I'm sorry, the auction is over. When I was called to conduct this auction, I was told of a secret stipulation in the will. I was not allowed to reveal that stipulation until this time. Only the painting of the son would be auctioned. Whoever bought that painting would inherit the entire estate, including the paintings. The man who took The Son gets everything!"

人群开始愤怒了，他们根本不想要那幅《儿子》的肖像。他们想为自己的收藏做更有价值的投资。竞拍师击槌，"10 美元一次，10 美元两次，10 美元成交。"第二排的一个男的嚷着："现在开始拍那些收藏品吧!"

竞拍师放下了小木槌。

"对不起，拍卖结束了。当我被召来主持这次拍卖时，我就被告知遗嘱中有一条秘密条款。在拍卖结束前不得透露，即只拍卖《儿子》的画像，不论是谁，只要买了这幅画就将继承所有的财产，包括那些画，谁要了《儿子》谁就得到所有一切。"

后 记

《白领英语轻悦读系列》是专门为广大英语爱好者编写的英语文章精品，精选了大量优秀的篇章，汇集了众多优秀的思想和智慧。本书全部采用中英文对照的形式，有助于广大的英语爱好者提高英语水平，希望能够给读者带来更多英语学习的乐趣和成果。

本书在编写过程中，查阅了大量的相关资料，并本着对读者负责的态度，在编译过程中也参考了其他译文中的经典、无法舍弃的佳句，由于受到了时间有限等诸多客观因素的制约，我们无法与部分资料的原作者取得联系，敬请谅解！在此特别向这些作者表示衷心的感谢，同时也请这些作者在读到本书后，尽快与编者取得联系。

联系方式：yingyushu2008@yahoo.com.cn

编者

2008 年 1 月